PAPERCUTZ SLICES

Harry Potty and the Deathly Boring

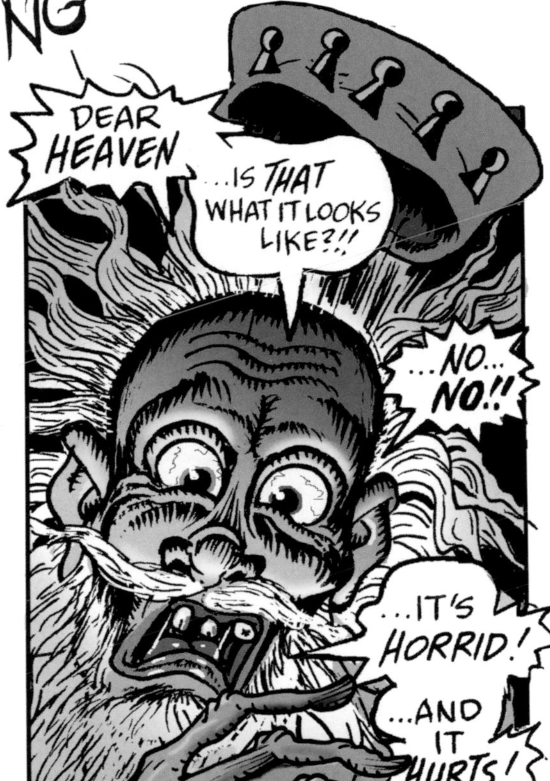
DEAR HEAVEN
...IS THAT WHAT IT LOOKS LIKE?!!
...NO... NO!!
...IT'S HORRID!
...AND IT HURTS!

PAPERCUTZ

PAPERCUTZ SLICES

Harry Potty

AND THE DEATHLY BORING

STEFAN PETRUCHA
Writer
RICK PARKER
Artist

PAPERCUTZ™

New York

"Harry Potty and the Deathly Boring"

STEFAN PETRUCHA – Writer
RICK PARKER – Artist

TROY HAHN
Production

MICHAEL PETRANEK
Associate Editor

JIM SALICRUP
Editor-in-Chief

ISBN: 978-1-59707-217-5 paperback edition
ISBN: 978-1-59707-218-2 hardcover edition

Printed in the US by Lifetouch Production, Inc.
5126 Forest Hills Ct.
Loves Park, IL 61111

Distributed by Macmillan

First Printing

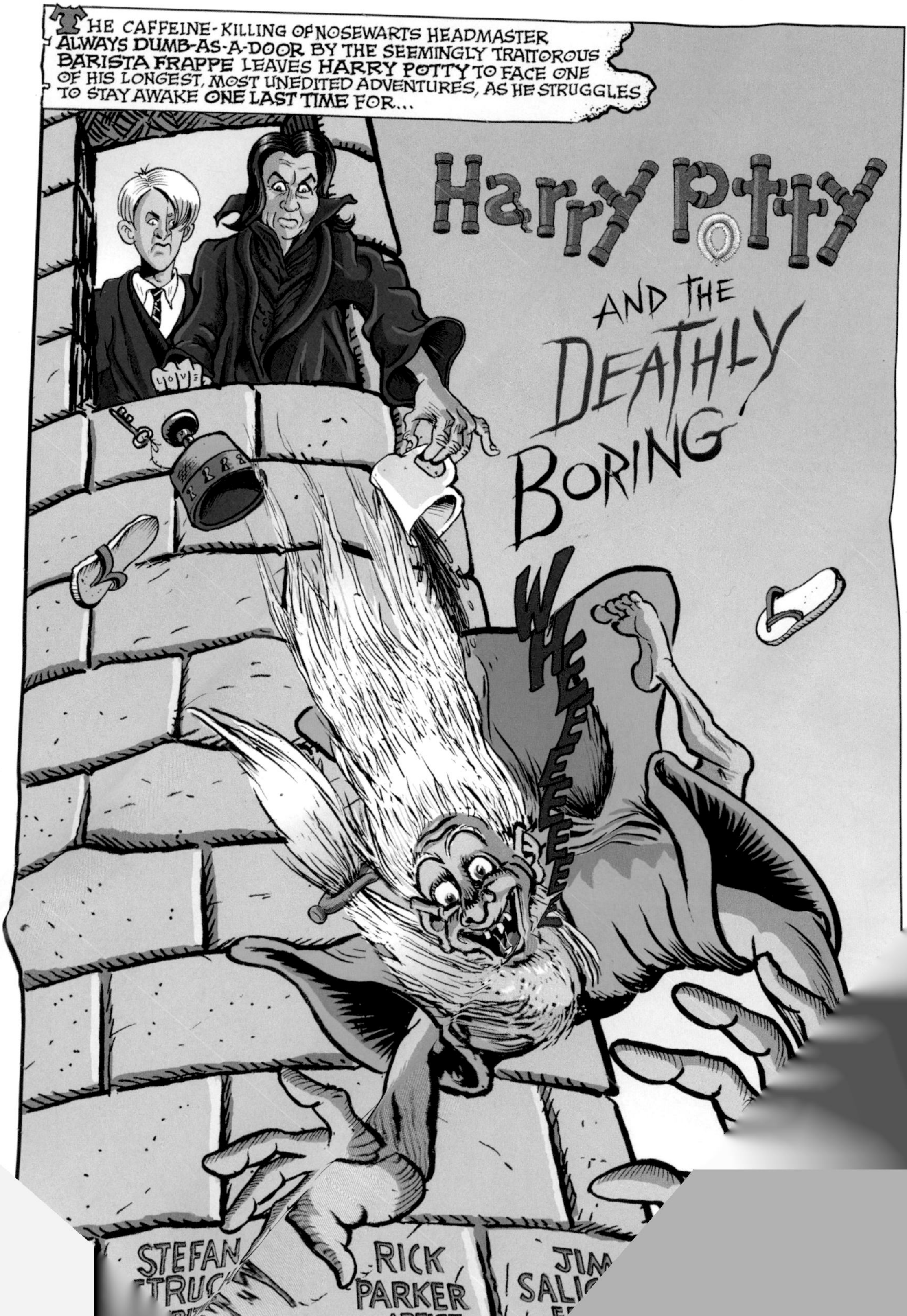
THE CAFFEINE-KILLING OF NOSEWARTS HEADMASTER ALWAYS DUMB-AS-A-DOOR BY THE SEEMINGLY TRAITOROUS BARISTA FRAPPE LEAVES HARRY POTTY TO FACE ONE OF HIS LONGEST, MOST UNEDITED ADVENTURES, AS HE STRUGGLES TO STAY AWAKE ONE LAST TIME FOR...
Harry Potty
AND THE DEATHLY BORING
STEFAN
RICK PARKER
ARTIST

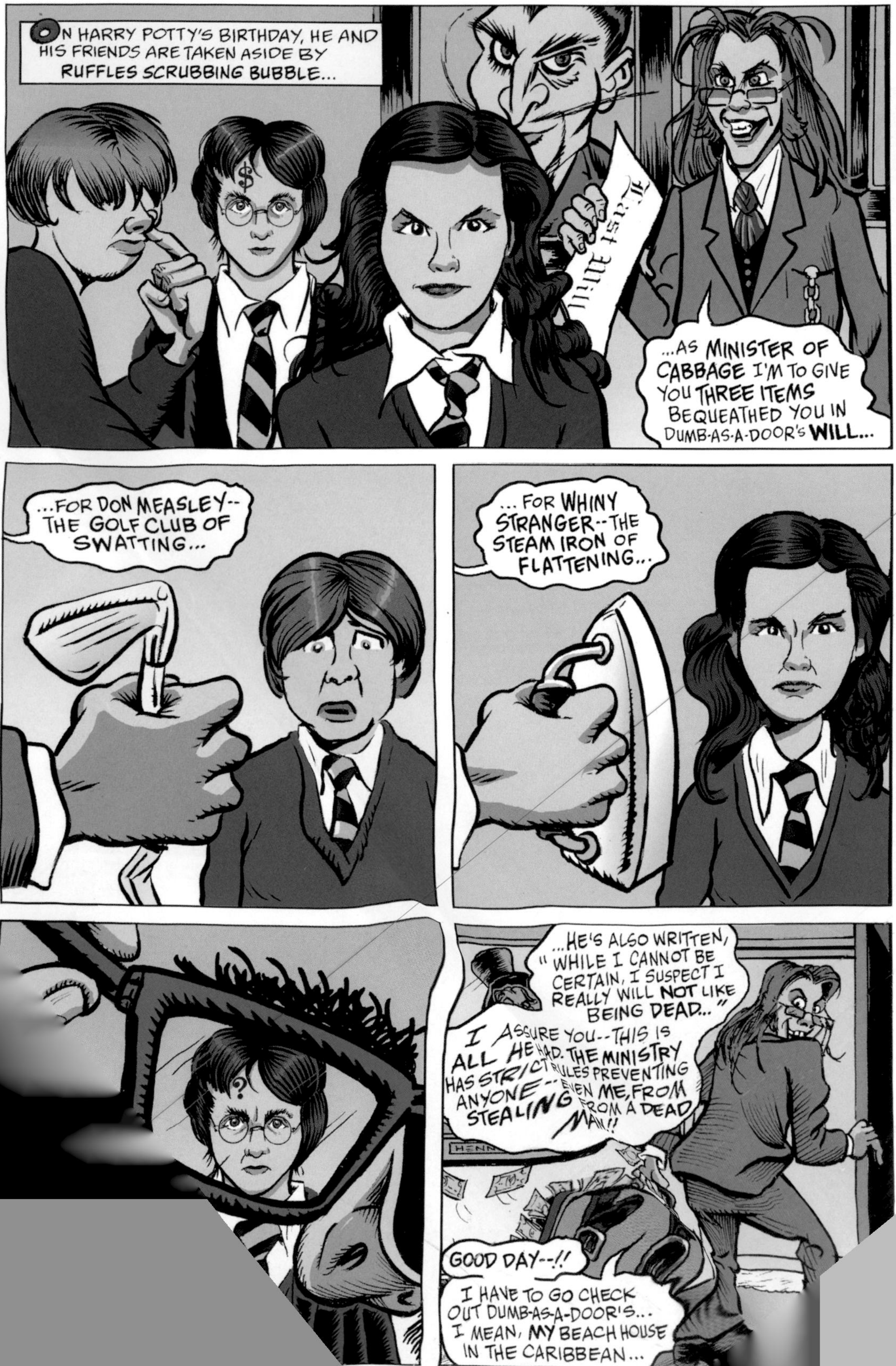
ON HARRY POTTY'S BIRTHDAY, HE AND HIS FRIENDS ARE TAKEN ASIDE BY RUFFLES SCRUBBING BUBBLE...
...AS MINISTER OF CABBAGE I'M TO GIVE YOU THREE ITEMS BEQUEATHED YOU IN DUMB-AS-A-DOOR'S WILL...
...FOR DON MEASLEY-- THE GOLF CLUB OF SWATTING...
... FOR WHINY STRANGER--THE STEAM IRON OF FLATTENING...
...HE'S ALSO WRITTEN, "WHILE I CANNOT BE CERTAIN, I SUSPECT I REALLY WILL NOT LIKE BEING DEAD..."
I ASSURE YOU--THIS IS ALL HE HAD. THE MINISTRY HAS STRICT RULES PREVENTING ANYONE--EVEN ME, FROM STEALING FROM A DEAD MAN!!
GOOD DAY--!!
I HAVE TO GO CHECK OUT DUMB-AS-A-DOOR'S... I MEAN, MY BEACH HOUSE IN THE CARIBBEAN...

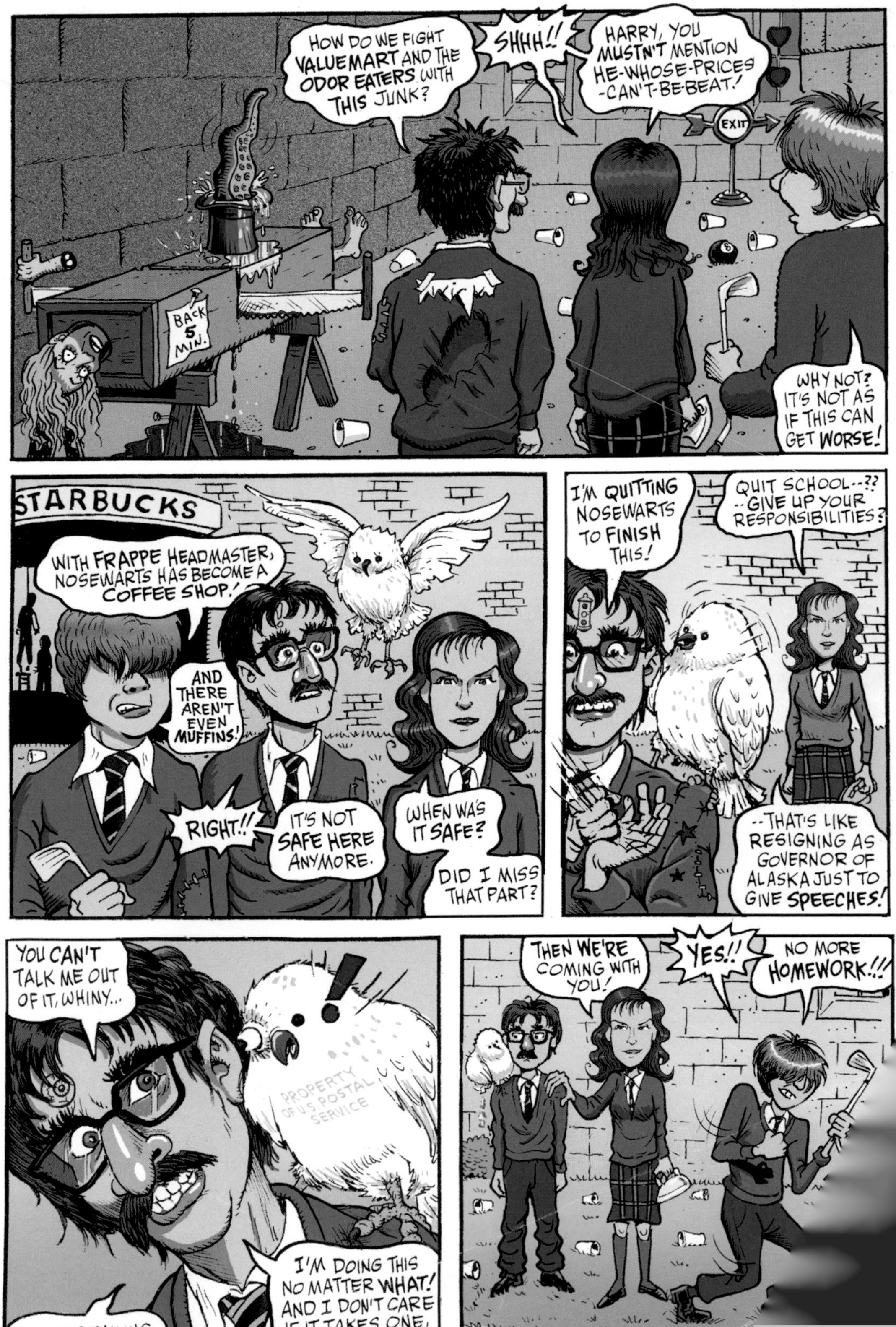
HOW DO WE FIGHT VALUEMART AND THE ODOR EATERS WITH THIS JUNK?
SHHH!!
HARRY, YOU MUSTN'T MENTION HE-WHOSE-PRICES-CAN'T-BE-BEAT!
EXIT
BACK 5 MIN.
WHY NOT? IT'S NOT AS IF THIS CAN GET WORSE!
STARBUCKS
WITH FRAPPE HEADMASTER, NOSEWARTS HAS BECOME A COFFEE SHOP!
AND THERE AREN'T EVEN MUFFINS!
RIGHT!!
IT'S NOT SAFE HERE ANYMORE.
WHEN WAS IT SAFE?
DID I MISS THAT PART?
I'M QUITTING NOSEWARTS TO FINISH THIS!
QUIT SCHOOL--?? --GIVE UP YOUR RESPONSIBILITIES?
--THAT'S LIKE RESIGNING AS GOVERNOR OF ALASKA JUST TO GIVE SPEECHES!
YOU CAN'T TALK ME OUT OF IT, WHINY...
!
PROPERTY OF U.S. POSTAL SERVICE
... I WAS FAILING ALL MY CLASSES ANYWAY...
I'M DOING THIS NO MATTER WHAT! AND I DON'T CARE IF IT TAKES ONE, TWO, OR EVEN THREE MOVIES!
THEN WE'RE COMING WITH YOU!
YES!!
NO MORE HOMEWORK!!!

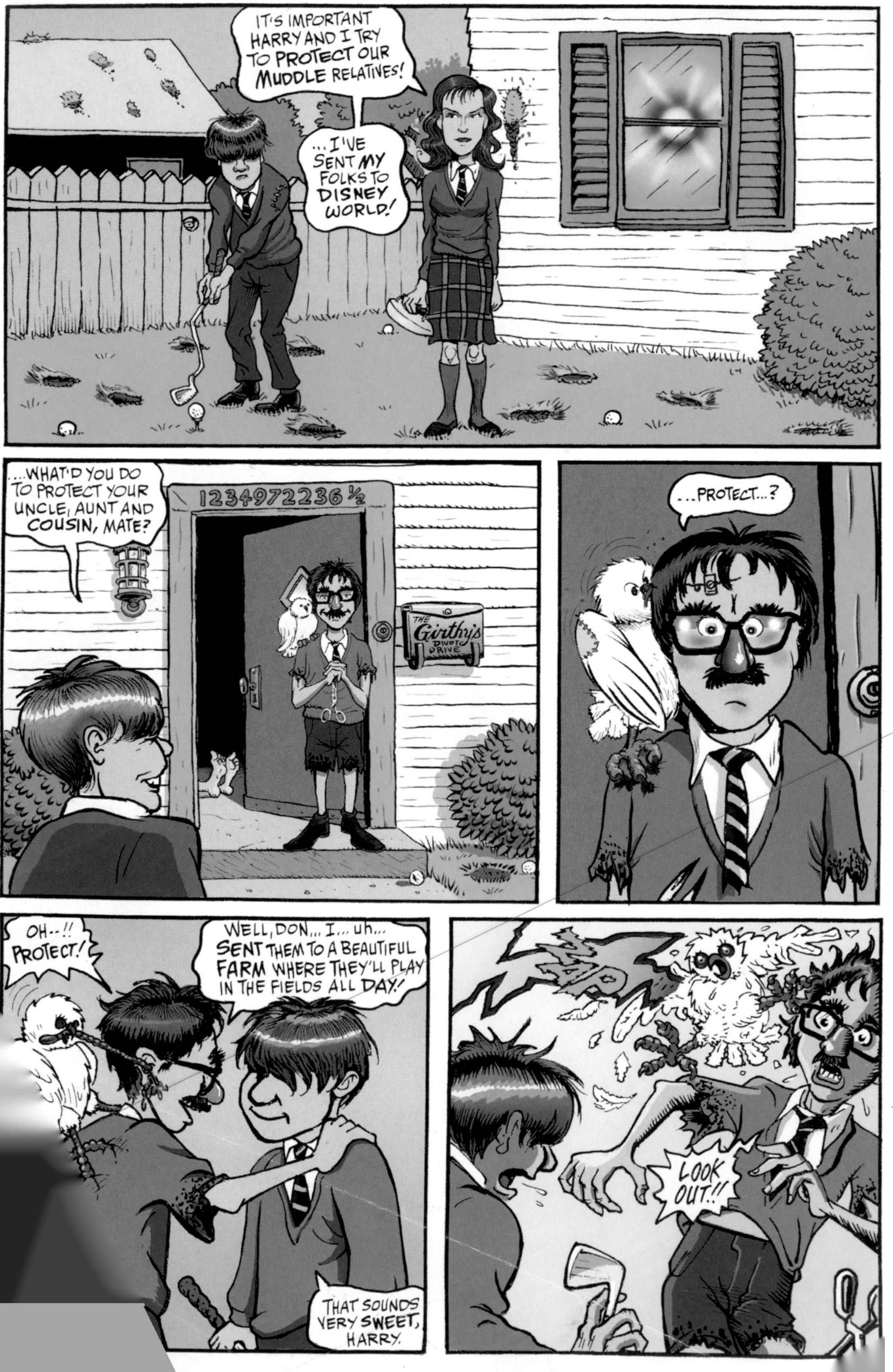
IT'S IMPORTANT HARRY AND I TRY TO PROTECT OUR MUDDLE RELATIVES!
...I'VE SENT MY FOLKS TO DISNEY WORLD!
...WHAT'D YOU DO TO PROTECT YOUR UNCLE, AUNT AND COUSIN, MATE?
1234972236 1/2
THE Girthy's DIVOT DRIVE
...PROTECT...?
OH--!! PROTECT!
WELL, DON... I... uh... SENT THEM TO A BEAUTIFUL FARM WHERE THEY'LL PLAY IN THE FIELDS ALL DAY!
THAT SOUNDS VERY SWEET, HARRY.
ZAP
LOOK OUT!!

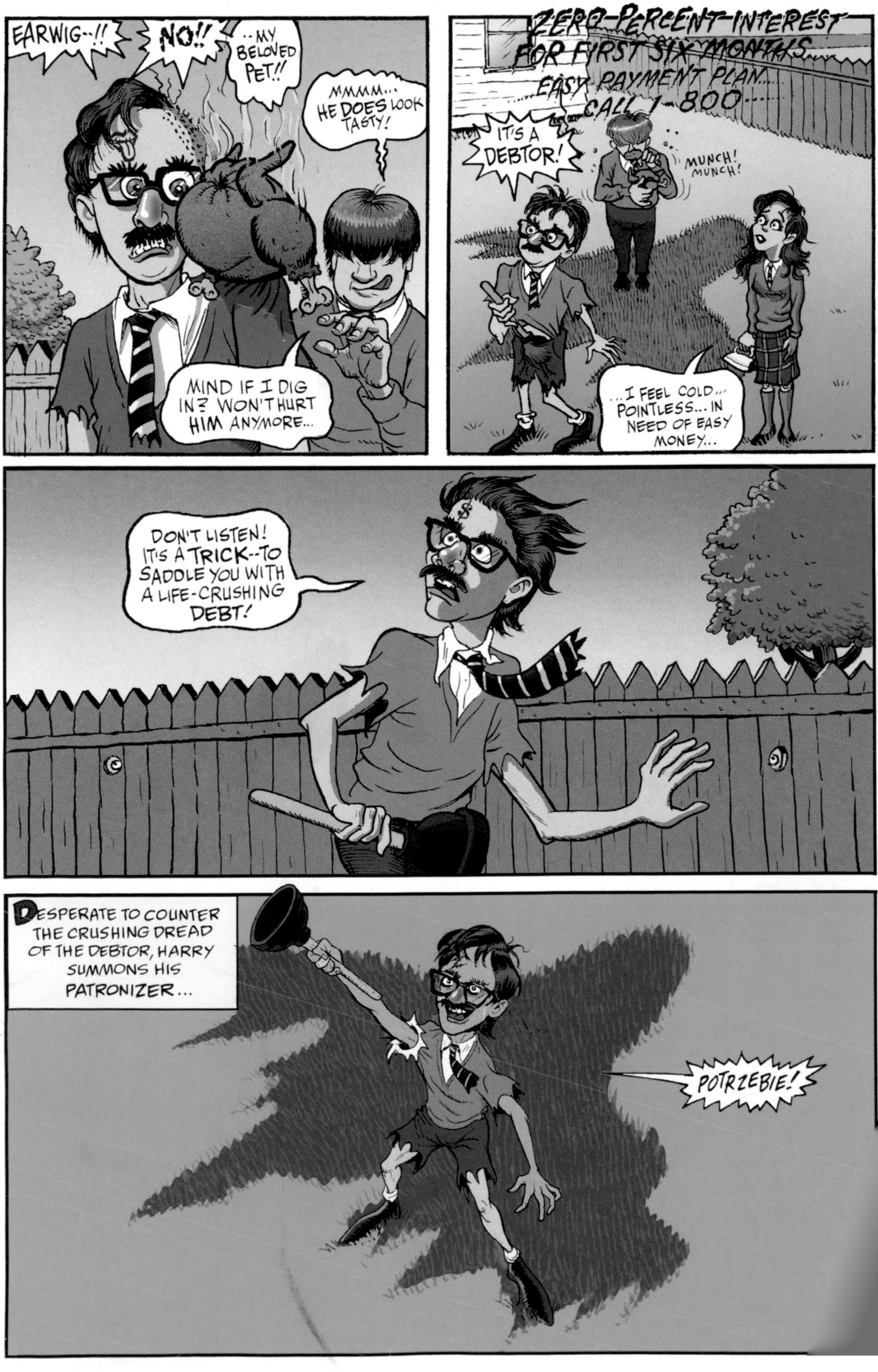
EARWIG--!!
NO!!
..MY BELOVED PET!!
MMMM... HE DOES LOOK TASTY!
MIND IF I DIG IN? WON'T HURT HIM ANYMORE...
ZERO-PERCENT INTEREST
FOR FIRST SIX MONTHS
EASY PAYMENT PLAN...
CALL 1-800...
IT'S A DEBTOR!
MUNCH! MUNCH!
...I FEEL COLD... POINTLESS... IN NEED OF EASY MONEY...
DON'T LISTEN! IT'S A TRICK--TO SADDLE YOU WITH A LIFE-CRUSHING DEBT!
DESPERATE TO COUNTER THE CRUSHING DREAD OF THE DEBTOR, HARRY SUMMONS HIS PATRONIZER...
POTRZEBIE!

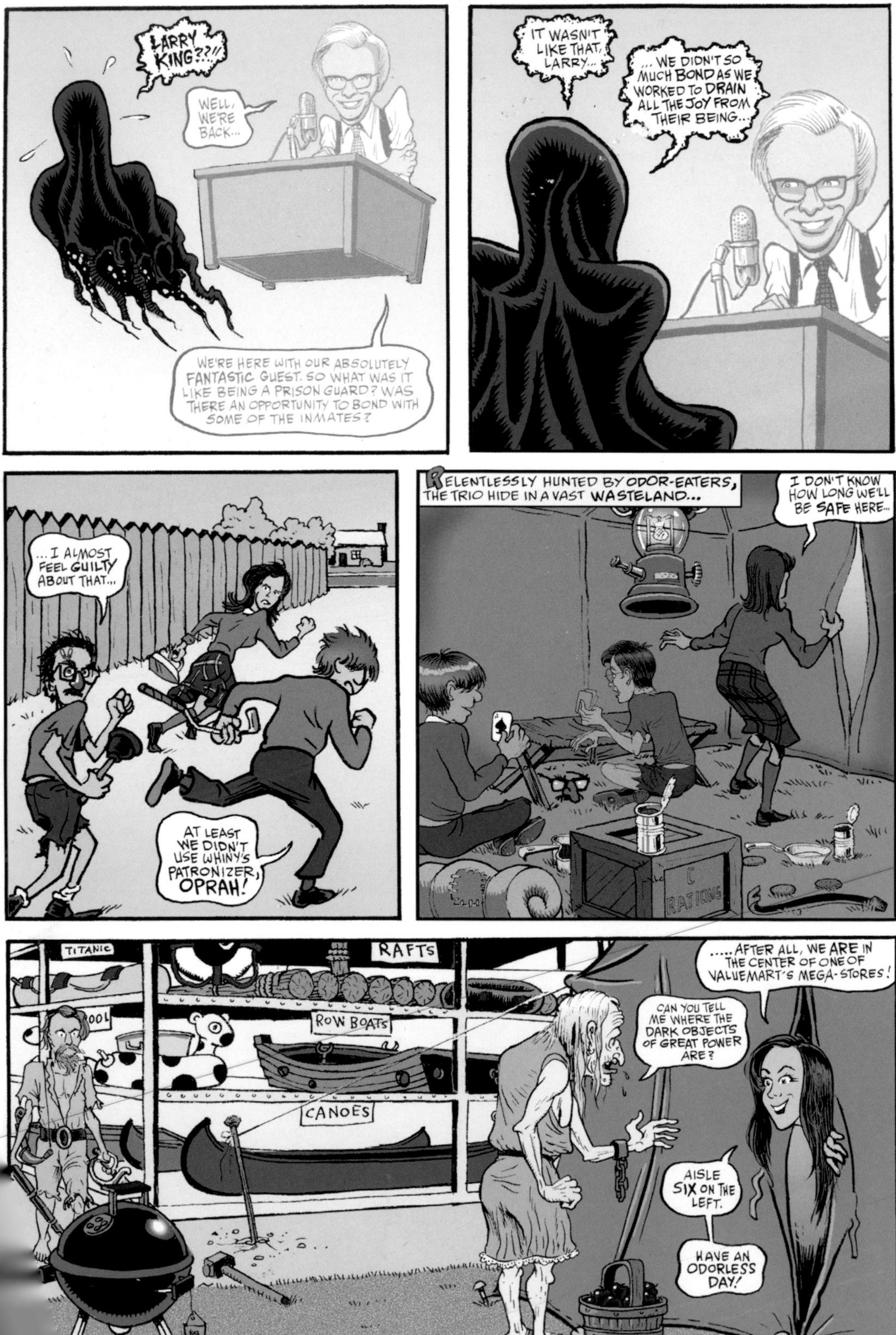
LARRY KING??!!
WELL, WE'RE BACK...
WE'RE HERE WITH OUR ABSOLUTELY FANTASTIC GUEST. SO WHAT WAS IT LIKE BEING A PRISON GUARD? WAS THERE AN OPPORTUNITY TO BOND WITH SOME OF THE INMATES?
IT WASN'T LIKE THAT, LARRY...
...WE DIDN'T SO MUCH BOND AS WE WORKED TO DRAIN ALL THE JOY FROM THEIR BEING...
...I ALMOST FEEL GUILTY ABOUT THAT...
AT LEAST WE DIDN'T USE WHINY'S PATRONIZER, OPRAH!
RELENTLESSLY HUNTED BY ODOR-EATERS, THE TRIO HIDE IN A VAST WASTELAND...
I DON'T KNOW HOW LONG WE'LL BE SAFE HERE...
C RATIONS
.....AFTER ALL, WE ARE IN THE CENTER OF ONE OF VALUEMART'S MEGA-STORES!
TITANIC
RAFTS
ROW BOATS
CANOES
CAN YOU TELL ME WHERE THE DARK OBJECTS OF GREAT POWER ARE?
AISLE SIX ON THE LEFT.
HAVE AN ODORLESS DAY!

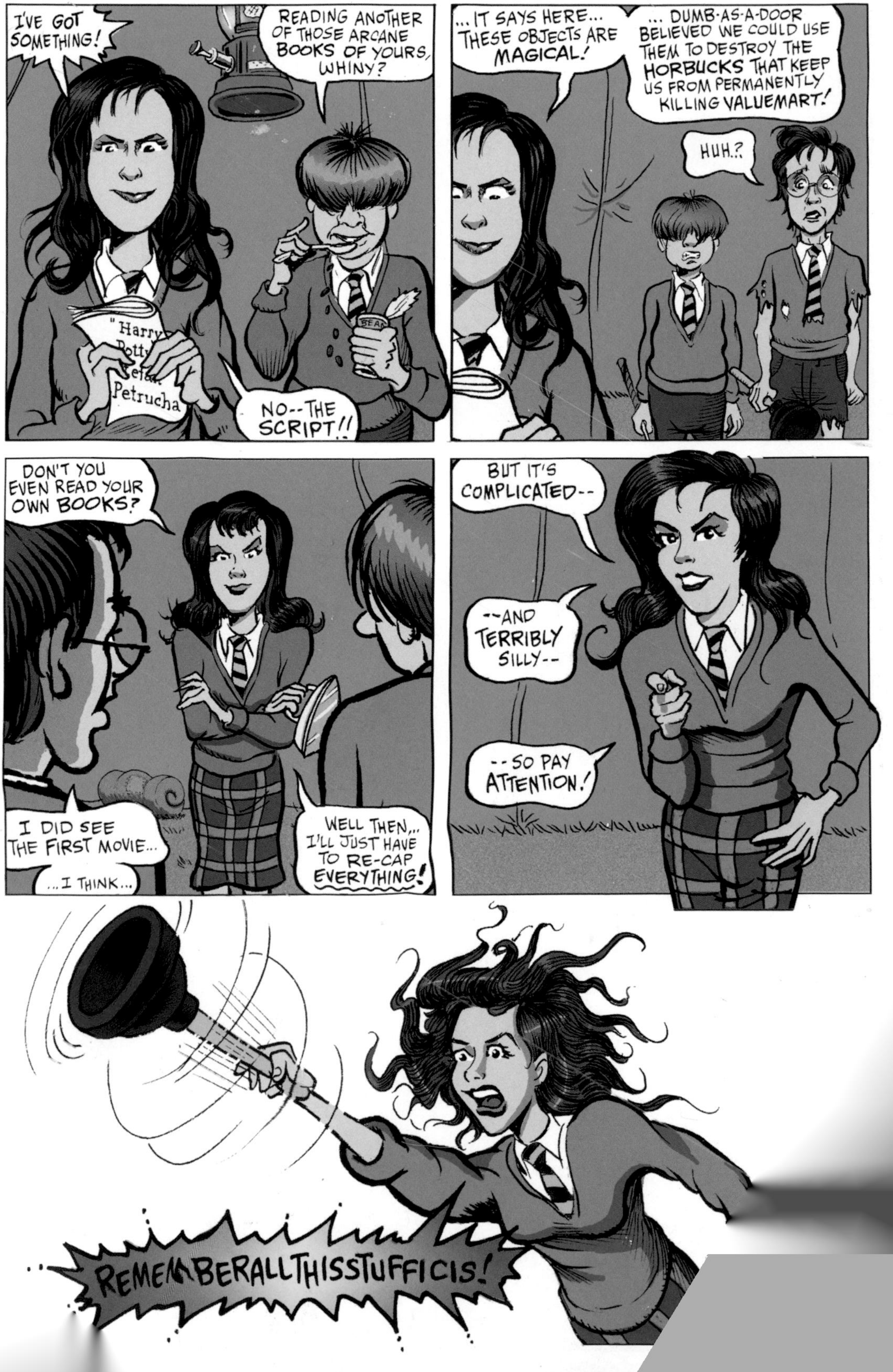
I'VE GOT SOMETHING!
READING ANOTHER OF THOSE ARCANE BOOKS OF YOURS, WHINY?
Harry
Petrucha
NO--THE SCRIPT!!
...IT SAYS HERE... THESE OBJECTS ARE MAGICAL!
...DUMB-AS-A-DOOR BELIEVED WE COULD USE THEM TO DESTROY THE HORBUCKS THAT KEEP US FROM PERMANENTLY KILLING VALUEMART!
HUH.?
DON'T YOU EVEN READ YOUR OWN BOOKS?
I DID SEE THE FIRST MOVIE...
...I THINK...
WELL THEN,,, I'LL JUST HAVE TO RE-CAP EVERYTHING!
BUT IT'S COMPLICATED--
--AND TERRIBLY SILLY--
--SO PAY ATTENTION!
REMEMBERALLTHISSTUFFICIS!

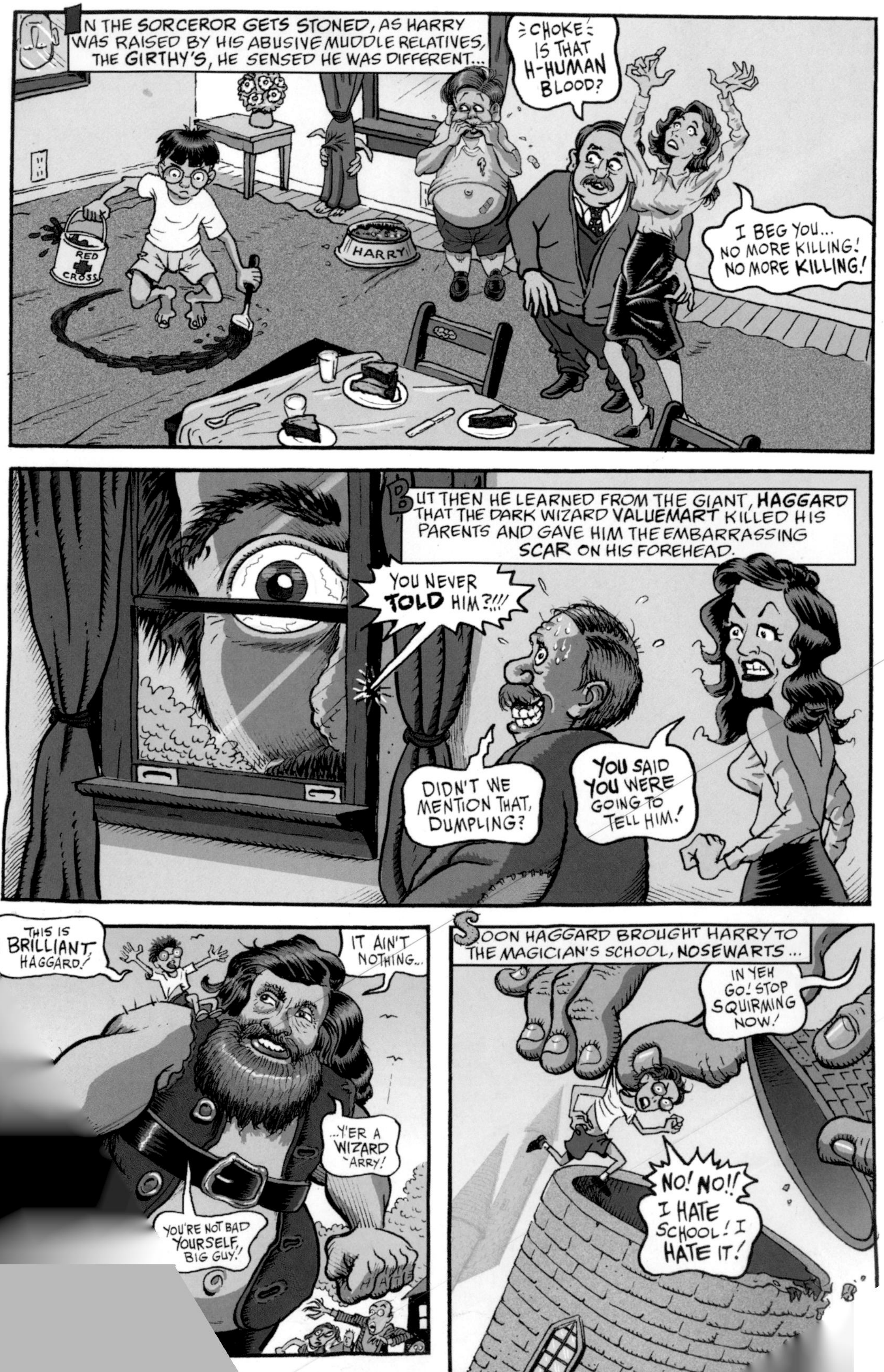
IN THE SORCEROR GETS STONED, AS HARRY WAS RAISED BY HIS ABUSIVE MUDDLE RELATIVES, THE GIRTHY'S, HE SENSED HE WAS DIFFERENT...
CHOKE IS THAT H-HUMAN BLOOD?
I BEG YOU... NO MORE KILLING! NO MORE KILLING!
RED CROSS
HARRY
BUT THEN HE LEARNED FROM THE GIANT, HAGGARD THAT THE DARK WIZARD VALUEMART KILLED HIS PARENTS AND GAVE HIM THE EMBARRASSING SCAR ON HIS FOREHEAD.
YOU NEVER TOLD HIM?!!!
DIDN'T WE MENTION THAT, DUMPLING?
YOU SAID YOU WERE GOING TO TELL HIM!
THIS IS BRILLIANT, HAGGARD!
IT AIN'T NOTHING...
...Y'ER A WIZARD 'ARRY!
YOU'RE NOT BAD YOURSELF, BIG GUY!
SOON HAGGARD BROUGHT HARRY TO THE MAGICIAN'S SCHOOL, NOSEWARTS...
IN YEH GO! STOP SQUIRMING NOW!
NO! NO!! I HATE SCHOOL! I HATE IT!

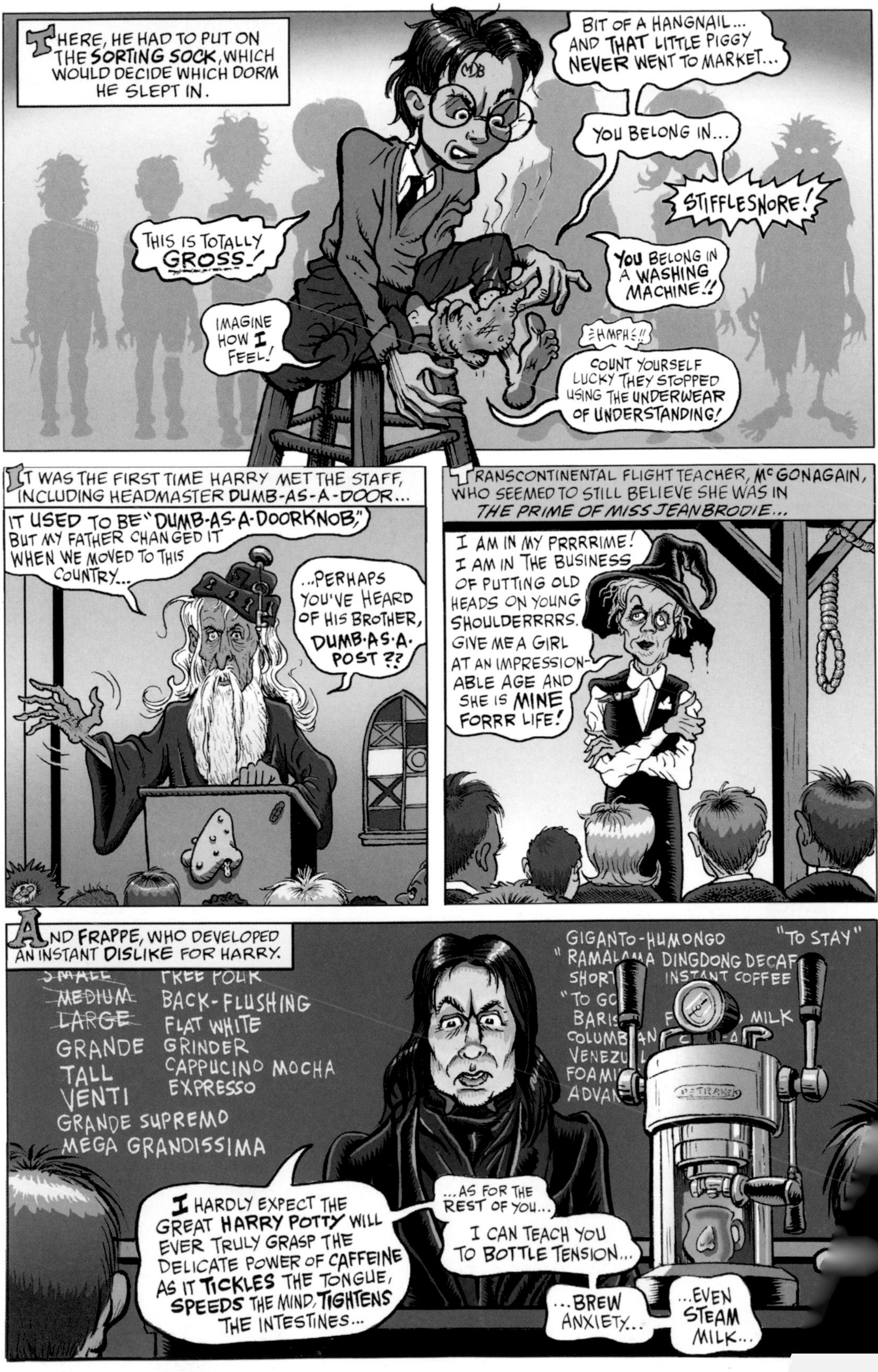
THERE, HE HAD TO PUT ON THE SORTING SOCK, WHICH WOULD DECIDE WHICH DORM HE SLEPT IN.
BIT OF A HANGNAIL... AND THAT LITTLE PIGGY NEVER WENT TO MARKET...
YOU BELONG IN...
STIFFLESNORE!
THIS IS TOTALLY GROSS!
YOU BELONG IN A WASHING MACHINE!!
IMAGINE HOW I FEEL!
EHMPH!!
COUNT YOURSELF LUCKY THEY STOPPED USING THE UNDERWEAR OF UNDERSTANDING!
IT WAS THE FIRST TIME HARRY MET THE STAFF, INCLUDING HEADMASTER DUMB-AS-A-DOOR...
IT USED TO BE "DUMB-AS-A-DOORKNOB," BUT MY FATHER CHANGED IT WHEN WE MOVED TO THIS COUNTRY...
...PERHAPS YOU'VE HEARD OF HIS BROTHER, DUMB-AS-A-POST??
TRANSCONTINENTAL FLIGHT TEACHER, McGONAGAIN, WHO SEEMED TO STILL BELIEVE SHE WAS IN THE PRIME OF MISS JEAN BRODIE...
I AM IN MY PRRRRIME! I AM IN THE BUSINESS OF PUTTING OLD HEADS ON YOUNG SHOULDERRRRS. GIVE ME A GIRL AT AN IMPRESSIONABLE AGE AND SHE IS MINE FORRR LIFE!
AND FRAPPE, WHO DEVELOPED AN INSTANT DISLIKE FOR HARRY.
MEDIUM
LARGE
GRANDE
TALL
VENTI
GRANDE SUPREMO
MEGA GRANDISSIMA
BACK-FLUSHING
FLAT WHITE
GRINDER
CAPPUCINO MOCHA
EXPRESSO
GIGANTO-HUMONGO
"TO STAY"
INSTANT COFFEE
I HARDLY EXPECT THE GREAT HARRY POTTY WILL EVER TRULY GRASP THE DELICATE POWER OF CAFFEINE AS IT TICKLES THE TONGUE, SPEEDS THE MIND, TIGHTENS THE INTESTINES...
...AS FOR THE REST OF YOU...
I CAN TEACH YOU TO BOTTLE TENSION...
...BREW ANXIETY...
...EVEN STEAM MILK...

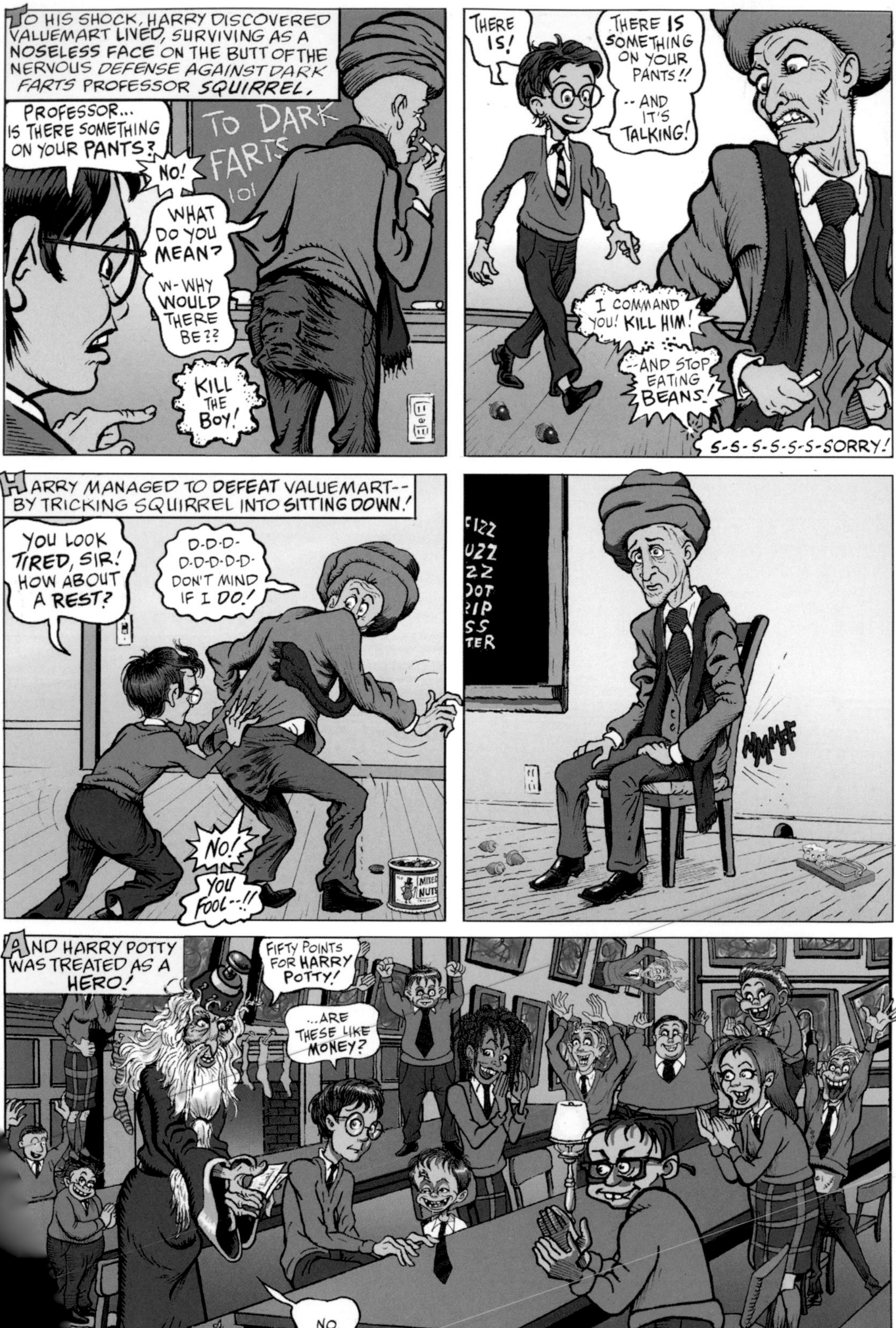
TO HIS SHOCK, HARRY DISCOVERED VALUEMART LIVED, SURVIVING AS A NOSELESS FACE ON THE BUTT OF THE NERVOUS DEFENSE AGAINST DARK FARTS PROFESSOR SQUIRREL.
TO DARK FARTS 101
PROFESSOR... IS THERE SOMETHING ON YOUR PANTS?
NO!
WHAT DO YOU MEAN?
W-WHY WOULD THERE BE??
KILL THE BOY!
THERE IS!
THERE IS SOMETHING ON YOUR PANTS!!
--AND IT'S TALKING!
I COMMAND YOU! KILL HIM!
--AND STOP EATING BEANS!
S-S-S-S-S-S-SORRY!
HARRY MANAGED TO DEFEAT VALUEMART-- BY TRICKING SQUIRREL INTO SITTING DOWN!
YOU LOOK TIRED, SIR! HOW ABOUT A REST?
D-D-D- D-D-D-D-D- DON'T MIND IF I DO!
NO!
YOU FOOL--!!
AND HARRY POTTY WAS TREATED AS A HERO!
FIFTY POINTS FOR HARRY POTTY!
...ARE THESE LIKE MONEY?
NO.

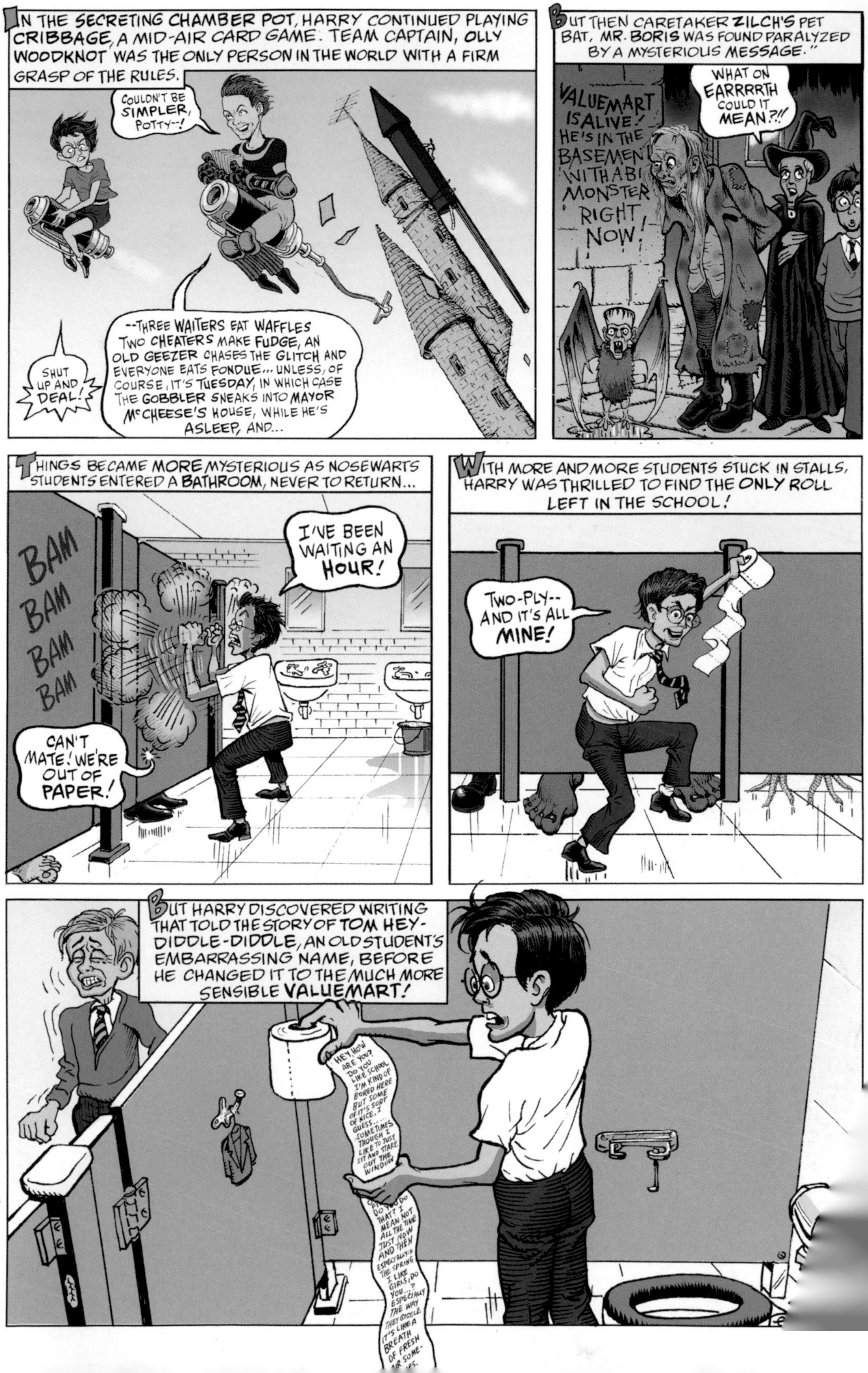

IN THE SECRETING CHAMBER POT, HARRY CONTINUED PLAYING CRIBBAGE, A MID-AIR CARD GAME. TEAM CAPTAIN, OLLY WOODKNOT WAS THE ONLY PERSON IN THE WORLD WITH A FIRM GRASP OF THE RULES.
COULDN'T BE SIMPLER, POTTY--!
--THREE WAITERS EAT WAFFLES TWO CHEATERS MAKE FUDGE, AN OLD GEEZER CHASES THE GLITCH AND EVERYONE EATS FONDUE... UNLESS, OF COURSE, IT'S TUESDAY, IN WHICH CASE THE GOBBLER SNEAKS INTO MAYOR McCHEESE'S HOUSE, WHILE HE'S ASLEEP, AND...
SHUT UP AND DEAL!
BUT THEN CARETAKER ZILCH'S PET BAT, MR. BORIS WAS FOUND PARALYZED BY A MYSTERIOUS MESSAGE."
VALUEMART IS ALIVE! HE'S IN THE BASEMENT WITH A BI MONSTER RIGHT NOW!
WHAT ON EARRRRTH COULD IT MEAN?!!
THINGS BECAME MORE MYSTERIOUS AS NOSEWARTS STUDENTS ENTERED A BATHROOM, NEVER TO RETURN...
BAM BAM BAM BAM
I'VE BEEN WAITING AN HOUR!
CAN'T MATE! WE'RE OUT OF PAPER!
WITH MORE AND MORE STUDENTS STUCK IN STALLS, HARRY WAS THRILLED TO FIND THE ONLY ROLL LEFT IN THE SCHOOL!
TWO-PLY-- AND IT'S ALL MINE!
BUT HARRY DISCOVERED WRITING THAT TOLD THE STORY OF TOM HEY-DIDDLE-DIDDLE, AN OLD STUDENT'S EMBARRASSING NAME, BEFORE HE CHANGED IT TO THE MUCH MORE SENSIBLE VALUEMART!
HEY, HOW ARE YOU? DO YOU LIKE SCHOOL I'M KIND OF BORED HERE BUT SOME OF IT'S SORT OF NICE, I GUESS...... SOMETIMES THOUGH I LIKE TO JUST SIT AND STARE OUT THE WINDOW
DO THAT? I MEAN NOT ALL THE TIME JUST NOW AND THEN ESPECIALLY IN THE SPRING I LIKE GIRLS, DO YOU...? ESPECIALLY THE WAY THEY GIGGLE IT'S LIKE A BREATH OF FRESH AIR SOME-

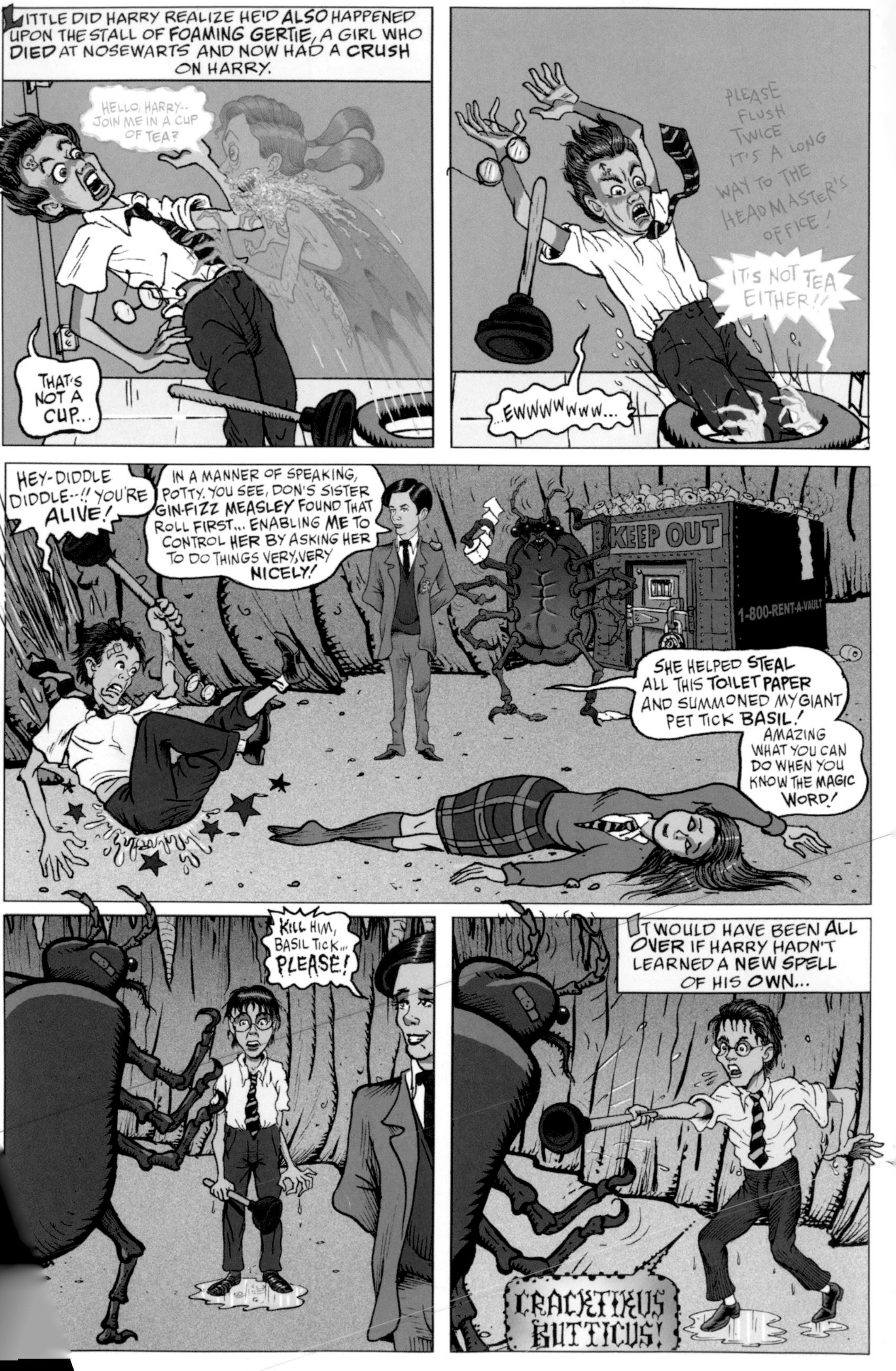
LITTLE DID HARRY REALIZE HE'D ALSO HAPPENED UPON THE STALL OF FOAMING GERTIE, A GIRL WHO DIED AT NOSEWARTS AND NOW HAD A CRUSH ON HARRY.
HELLO, HARRY.. JOIN ME IN A CUP OF TEA?
THAT'S NOT A CUP...
PLEASE FLUSH TWICE IT'S A LONG WAY TO THE HEADMASTER'S OFFICE!
IT'S NOT TEA EITHER!!
...EWWWWWWW...
HEY-DIDDLE DIDDLE--!! YOU'RE ALIVE!
IN A MANNER OF SPEAKING, POTTY. YOU SEE, DON'S SISTER GIN-FIZZ MEASLEY FOUND THAT ROLL FIRST... ENABLING ME TO CONTROL HER BY ASKING HER TO DO THINGS VERY, VERY NICELY!
KEEP OUT
1-800-RENT-A-VAULT
SHE HELPED STEAL ALL THIS TOILET PAPER AND SUMMONED MY GIANT PET TICK BASIL!
AMAZING WHAT YOU CAN DO WHEN YOU KNOW THE MAGIC WORD!
KILL HIM, BASIL TICK... PLEASE!
IT WOULD HAVE BEEN ALL OVER IF HARRY HADN'T LEARNED A NEW SPELL OF HIS OWN...
CRACKTIKUS BUTTICUS!

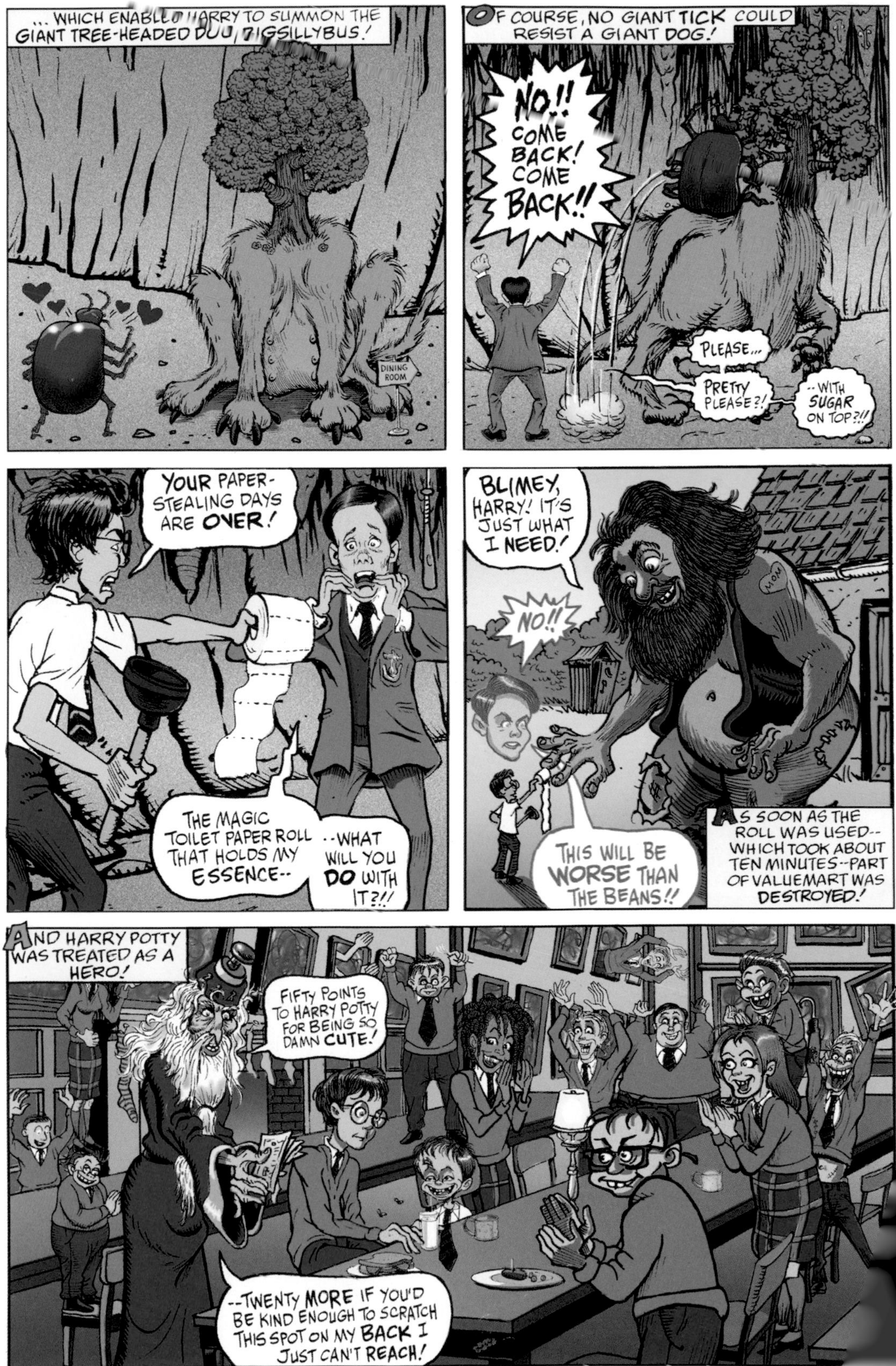
... WHICH ENABLED HARRY TO SUMMON THE GIANT TREE-HEADED DOG, ZIGSILLYBUS!
DINING ROOM
OF COURSE, NO GIANT TICK COULD RESIST A GIANT DOG!
NO!! COME BACK! COME BACK!!
PLEASE...
PRETTY PLEASE?!
--WITH SUGAR ON TOP?!!
YOUR PAPER-STEALING DAYS ARE OVER!
THE MAGIC TOILET PAPER ROLL THAT HOLDS MY ESSENCE--
--WHAT WILL YOU DO WITH IT?!!
BLIMEY, HARRY! IT'S JUST WHAT I NEED!
MOM
NO!!
THIS WILL BE WORSE THAN THE BEANS!!
AS SOON AS THE ROLL WAS USED--WHICH TOOK ABOUT TEN MINUTES--PART OF VALUEMART WAS DESTROYED!
AND HARRY POTTY WAS TREATED AS A HERO!
FIFTY POINTS TO HARRY POTTY FOR BEING SO DAMN CUTE!
--TWENTY MORE IF YOU'D BE KIND ENOUGH TO SCRATCH THIS SPOT ON MY BACK I JUST CAN'T REACH!

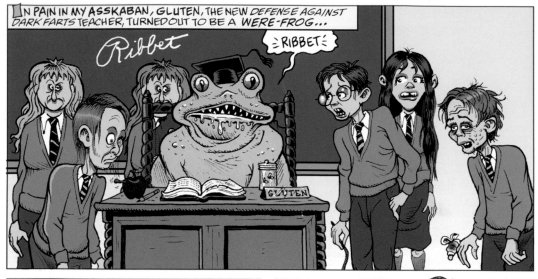

IN PAIN IN MY ASSKABAN, GLUTEN, THE NEW *DEFENSE AGAINST DARK FARTS* TEACHER, TURNED OUT TO BE A *WERE-FROG...*

RIBBET

≡RIBBET≡

MEANWHILE, SERIOUSLY BLACK, THE MAN ACCUSED OF BETRAYING HARRY'S PARENTS AND **KILLING** THEIR FRIEND, PETER PIPER, ESCAPED FROM PRISON!

YOUR DAD WAS MY *PAL!*

WAS HE?

IT TURNED OUT SERIOUSLY WAS WRONGLY ACCUSED. IT WAS PETER PIPER WHO BETRAYED HARRY'S PARENTS!

AND HE LOST *YOU* TO *ME* IN A *POKER GAME!*

DID HE...?

SO *YOU* HAVE TO DO *EVERYTHING* I SAY!

NO, SERIOUSLY...

NO, SERIOUSLY, SIR!

ONLY PIPER WASN'T EVEN DEAD! FOR YEARS HE LIVED DISGUISED AS DON'S CHEAP SECOND HAND, GIVEN HIM BY HIS POOR PARENTS. GET IT-? SECOND-HAND?

AH!

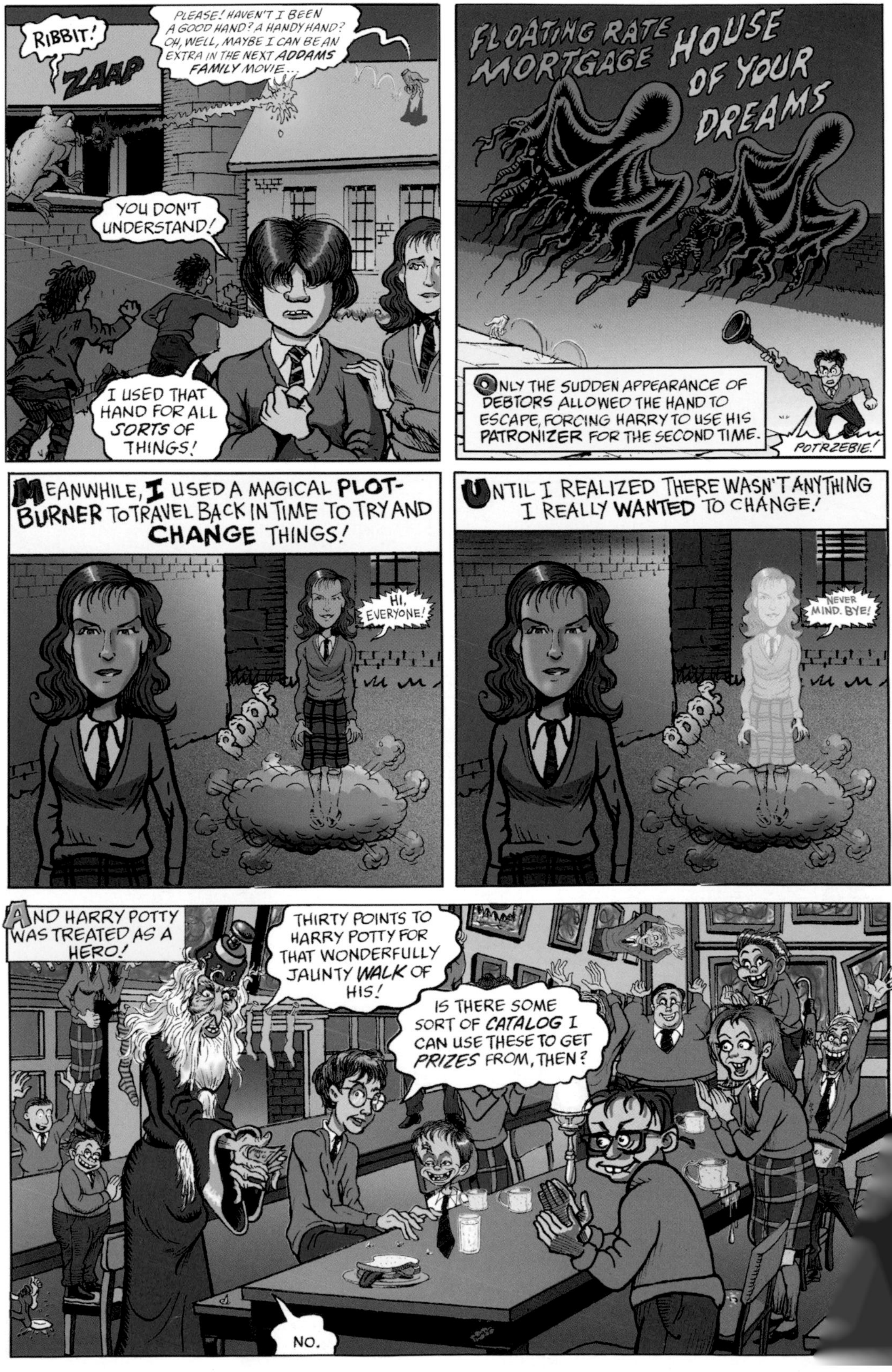

RIBBIT!
ZAAP
PLEASE! HAVEN'T I BEEN A GOOD HAND? A HANDY HAND? OH, WELL, MAYBE I CAN BE AN EXTRA IN THE NEXT ADDAMS FAMILY MOVIE...
YOU DON'T UNDERSTAND!
I USED THAT HAND FOR ALL SORTS OF THINGS!
FLOATING RATE MORTGAGE HOUSE OF YOUR DREAMS
ONLY THE SUDDEN APPEARANCE OF DEBTORS ALLOWED THE HAND TO ESCAPE, FORCING HARRY TO USE HIS PATRONIZER FOR THE SECOND TIME.
POTRZEBIE!
MEANWHILE, I USED A MAGICAL PLOT-BURNER TO TRAVEL BACK IN TIME TO TRY AND CHANGE THINGS!
HI, EVERYONE!
POOF
UNTIL I REALIZED THERE WASN'T ANYTHING I REALLY WANTED TO CHANGE!
NEVER MIND. BYE!
POOF
AND HARRY POTTY WAS TREATED AS A HERO!
THIRTY POINTS TO HARRY POTTY FOR THAT WONDERFULLY JAUNTY WALK OF HIS!
IS THERE SOME SORT OF CATALOG I CAN USE THESE TO GET PRIZES FROM, THEN?
NO.

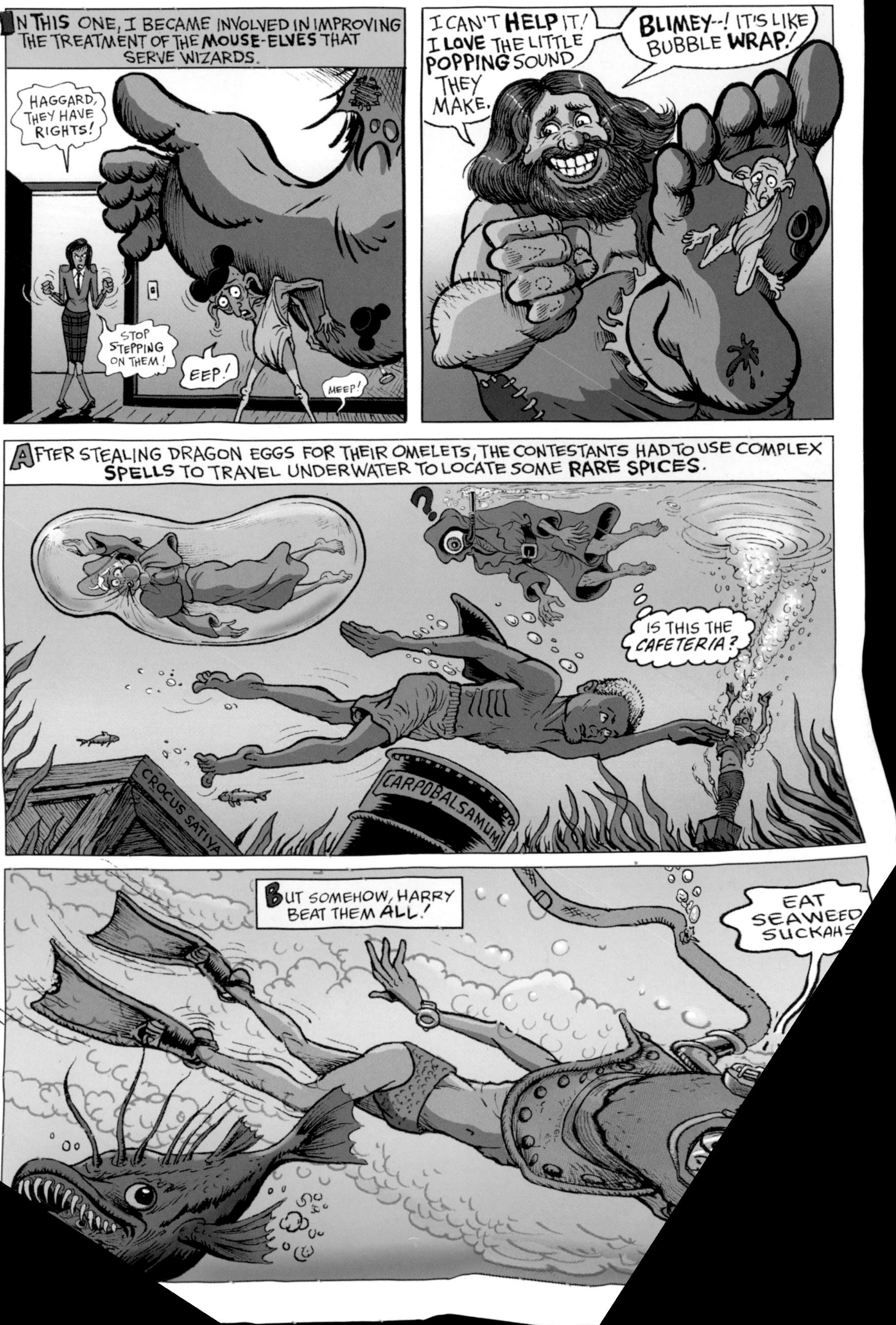
IN THIS ONE, I BECAME INVOLVED IN IMPROVING THE TREATMENT OF THE MOUSE-ELVES THAT SERVE WIZARDS.
HAGGARD, THEY HAVE RIGHTS!
STOP STEPPING ON THEM!
EEP!
MEEP!
I CAN'T HELP IT! I LOVE THE LITTLE POPPING SOUND THEY MAKE.
BLIMEY--! IT'S LIKE BUBBLE WRAP!
AFTER STEALING DRAGON EGGS FOR THEIR OMELETS, THE CONTESTANTS HAD TO USE COMPLEX SPELLS TO TRAVEL UNDERWATER TO LOCATE SOME RARE SPICES.
?
IS THIS THE CAFETERIA?
CROCUS SATIVA
CARPOBALSAMUM
BUT SOMEHOW, HARRY BEAT THEM ALL!
EAT SEAWEED SUCKAHS

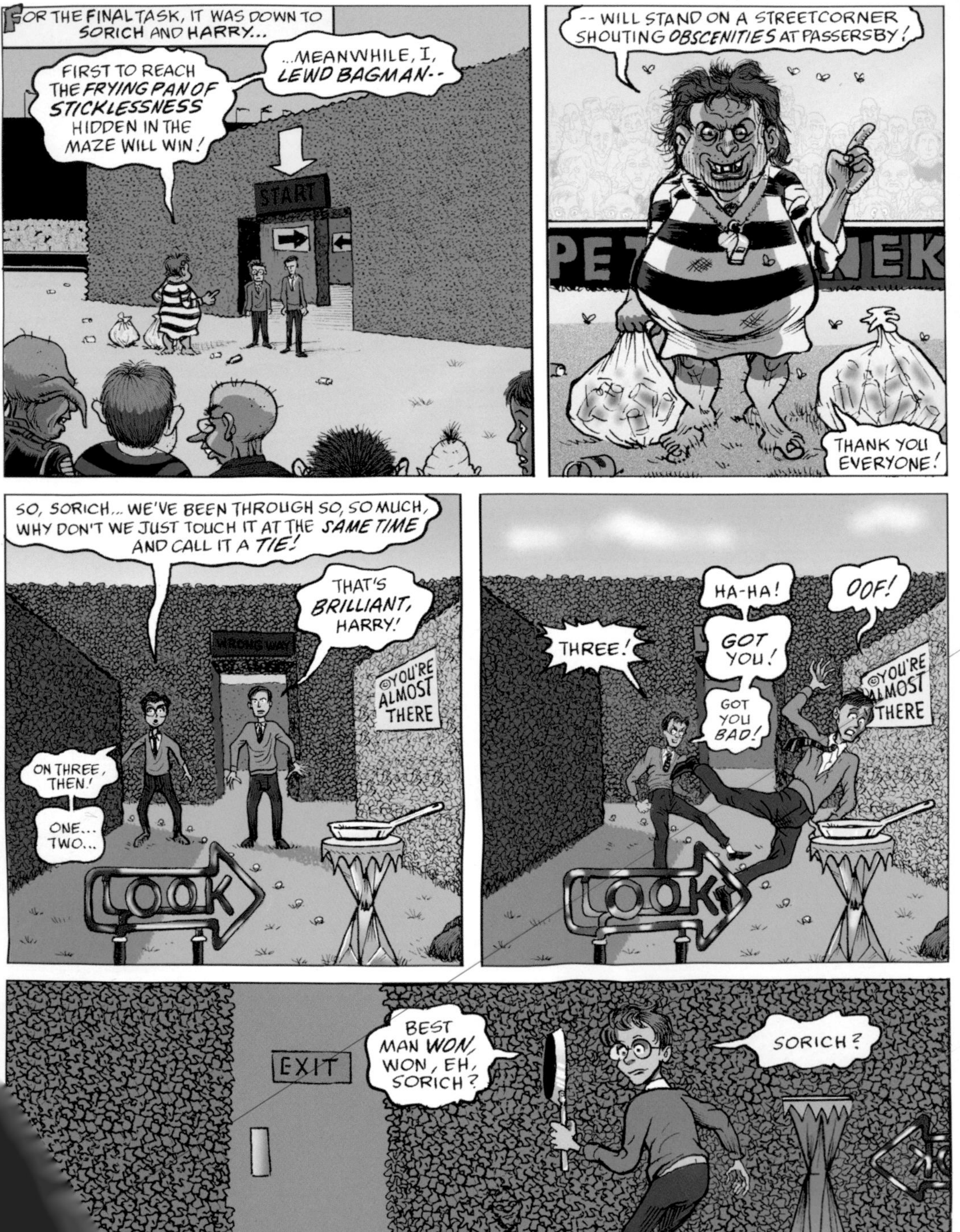
FOR THE FINAL TASK, IT WAS DOWN TO SORICH AND HARRY...
FIRST TO REACH THE FRYING PAN OF STICKLESSNESS HIDDEN IN THE MAZE WILL WIN!
...MEANWHILE, I, LEWD BAGMAN--
START
-- WILL STAND ON A STREETCORNER SHOUTING OBSCENITIES AT PASSERSBY!
THANK YOU EVERYONE!
SO, SORICH... WE'VE BEEN THROUGH SO, SO MUCH, WHY DON'T WE JUST TOUCH IT AT THE SAME TIME AND CALL IT A TIE!
THAT'S BRILLIANT, HARRY!
WRONG WAY
YOU'RE ALMOST THERE
ON THREE, THEN!
ONE... TWO...
LOOK
THREE!
HA-HA!
GOT YOU!
GOT YOU BAD!
OOF!
YOU'RE ALMOST THERE
LOOK
EXIT
BEST MAN WON, WON, EH, SORICH?
SORICH?

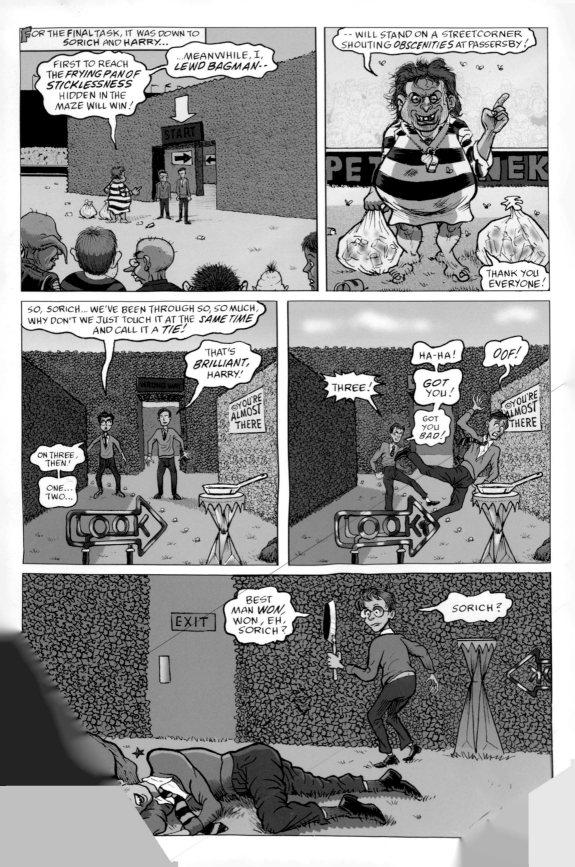

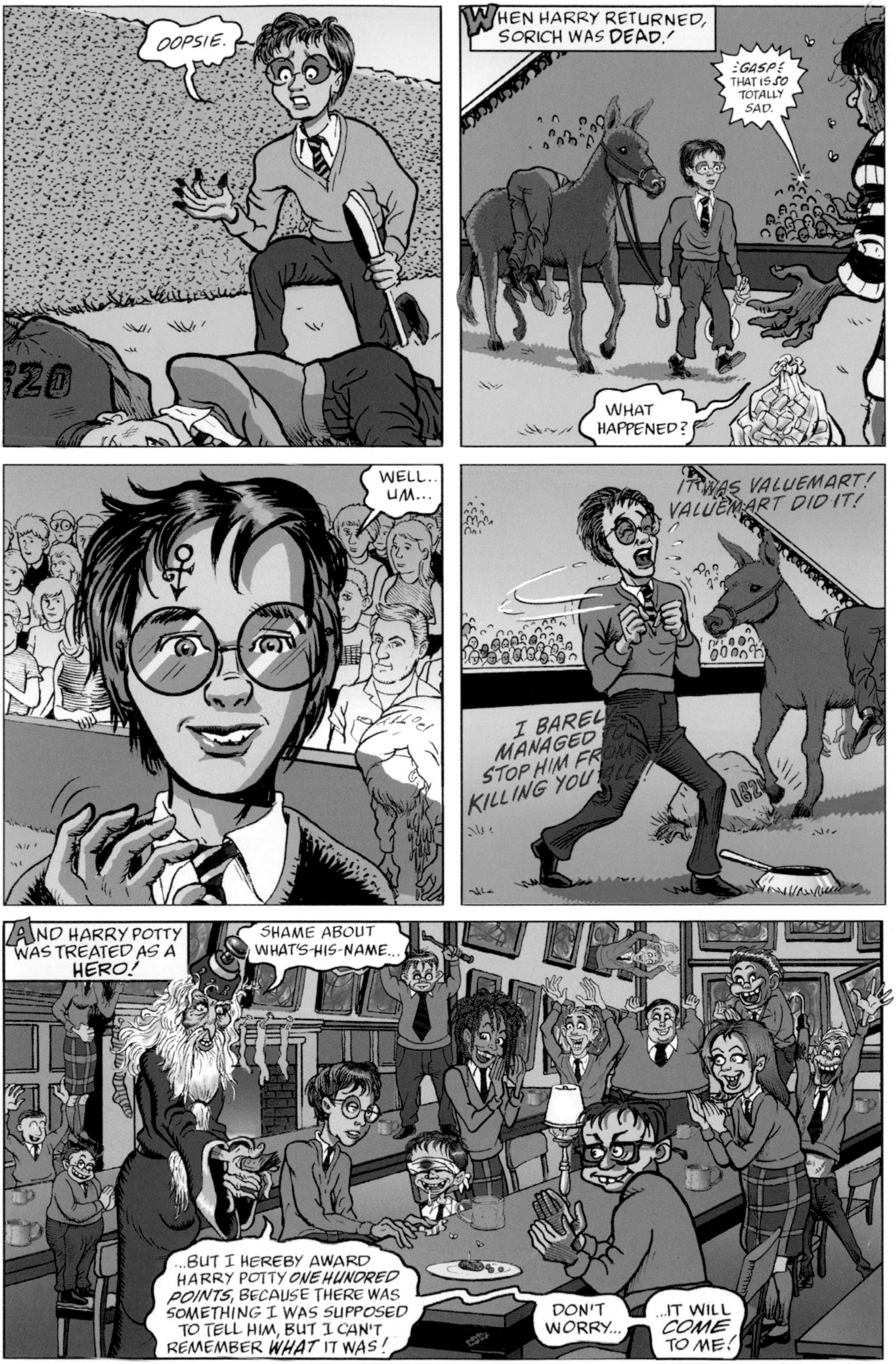
OOPSIE.
WHEN HARRY RETURNED, SORICH WAS DEAD!
GASP THAT IS SO TOTALLY SAD.
WHAT HAPPENED?
WELL.. UM...
IT WAS VALUEMART! VALUEMART DID IT!
I BARELY MANAGED TO STOP HIM FROM KILLING YOU ALL!
AND HARRY POTTY WAS TREATED AS A HERO!
SHAME ABOUT WHAT'S-HIS-NAME...
...BUT I HEREBY AWARD HARRY POTTY ONE HUNDRED POINTS, BECAUSE THERE WAS SOMETHING I WAS SUPPOSED TO TELL HIM, BUT I CAN'T REMEMBER WHAT IT WAS!
DON'T WORRY...
...IT WILL COME TO ME!

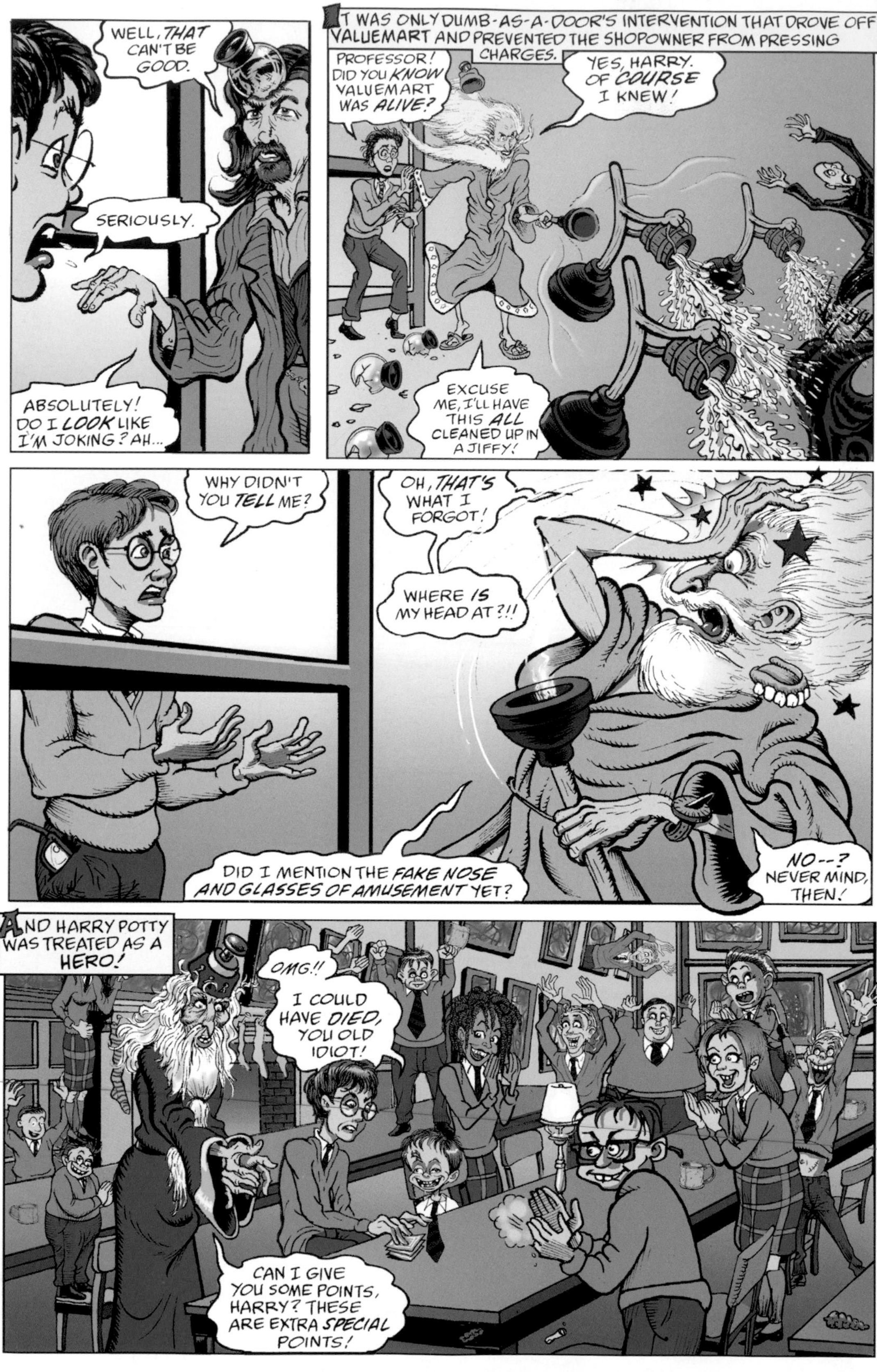
WELL, *THAT* CAN'T BE GOOD.
SERIOUSLY.
ABSOLUTELY! DO I *LOOK* LIKE I'M JOKING? AH...
IT WAS ONLY DUMB-AS-A-DOOR'S INTERVENTION THAT DROVE OFF VALUEMART AND PREVENTED THE SHOPOWNER FROM PRESSING CHARGES.
PROFESSOR! DID YOU *KNOW* VALUEMART WAS *ALIVE*?
YES, HARRY. OF *COURSE* I KNEW!
EXCUSE ME, I'LL HAVE THIS *ALL* CLEANED UP IN A JIFFY!
WHY DIDN'T YOU *TELL* ME?
OH, *THAT'S* WHAT I FORGOT!
WHERE *IS* MY HEAD AT?!!
DID I MENTION THE *FAKE NOSE AND GLASSES OF AMUSEMENT* YET?
NO--? NEVER MIND, THEN!
AND HARRY POTTY WAS TREATED AS A **HERO!**
OMG!! I COULD HAVE *DIED*, YOU OLD IDIOT!
CAN I GIVE YOU SOME POINTS, HARRY? THESE ARE EXTRA *SPECIAL* POINTS!

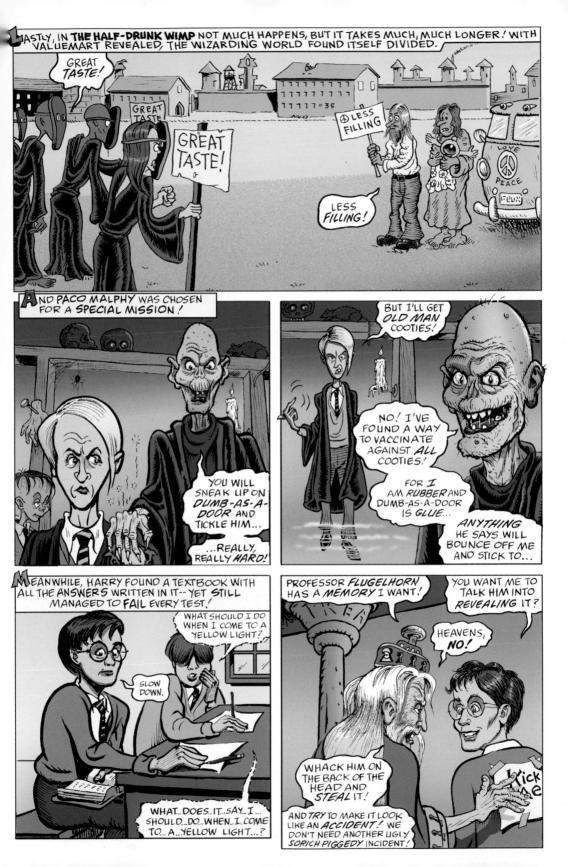

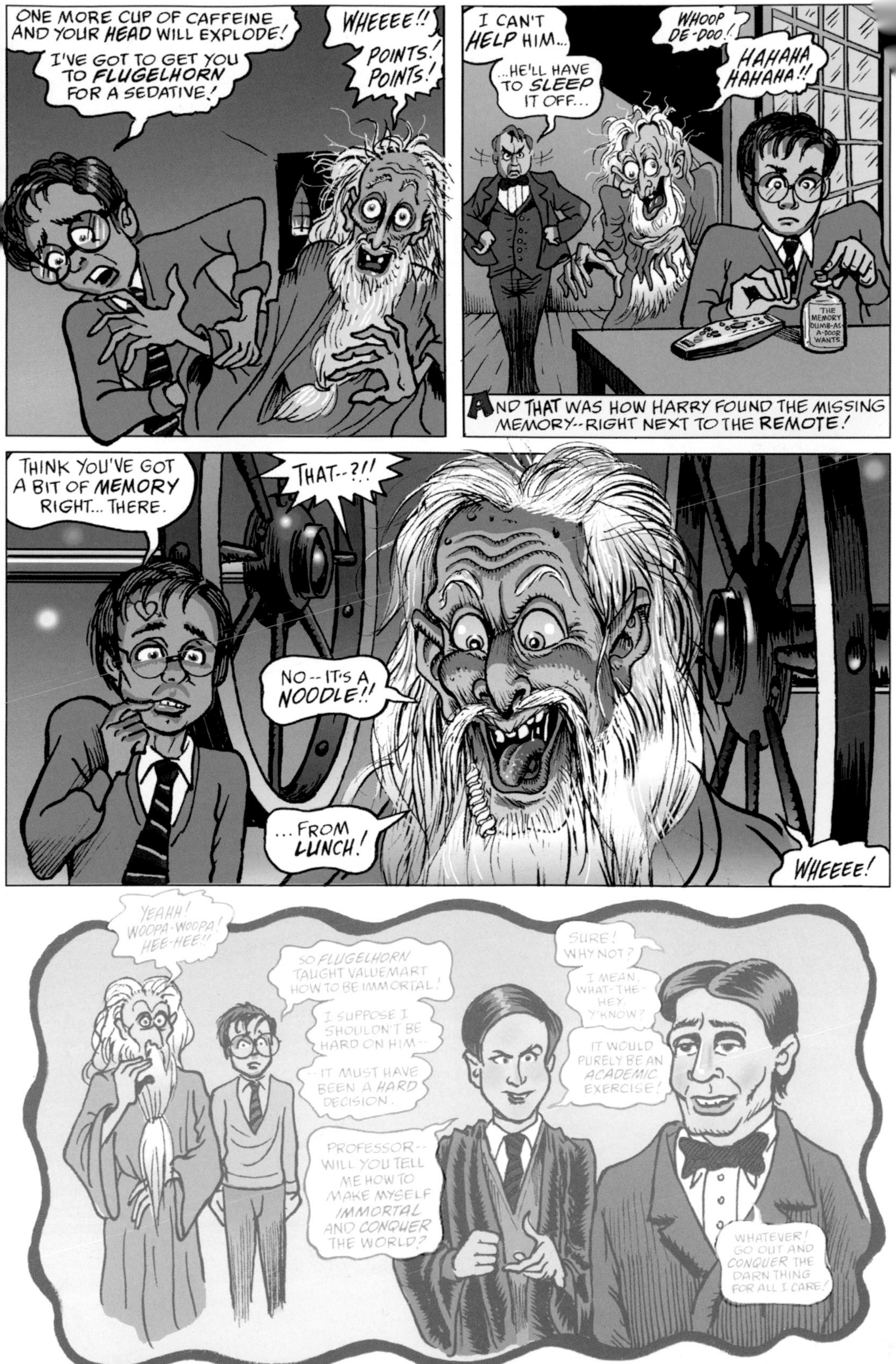
ONE MORE CUP OF CAFFEINE AND YOUR HEAD WILL EXPLODE!
I'VE GOT TO GET YOU TO FLUGELHORN FOR A SEDATIVE!
WHEEEE!!
POINTS! POINTS!
I CAN'T HELP HIM...
...HE'LL HAVE TO SLEEP IT OFF...
WHOOP DE-DOO!
HAHAHA HAHAHA!!
THE MEMORY DUMB-AS-A-DOOR WANTS
AND THAT WAS HOW HARRY FOUND THE MISSING MEMORY--RIGHT NEXT TO THE REMOTE!
THINK YOU'VE GOT A BIT OF MEMORY RIGHT... THERE.
THAT--?!!
NO--IT'S A NOODLE!!
...FROM LUNCH!
WHEEEE!
YEAHH! WOOPA-WOOPA! HEE-HEE!!
SO FLUGELHORN TAUGHT VALUEMART HOW TO BE IMMORTAL!
I SUPPOSE I SHOULDN'T BE HARD ON HIM--
--IT MUST HAVE BEEN A HARD DECISION.
PROFESSOR--WILL YOU TELL ME HOW TO MAKE MYSELF IMMORTAL AND CONQUER THE WORLD?
SURE! WHY NOT?
I MEAN, WHAT-THE-HEY, Y'KNOW?
IT WOULD PURELY BE AN ACADEMIC EXERCISE!
WHATEVER! GO OUT AND CONQUER THE DARN THING FOR ALL I CARE!

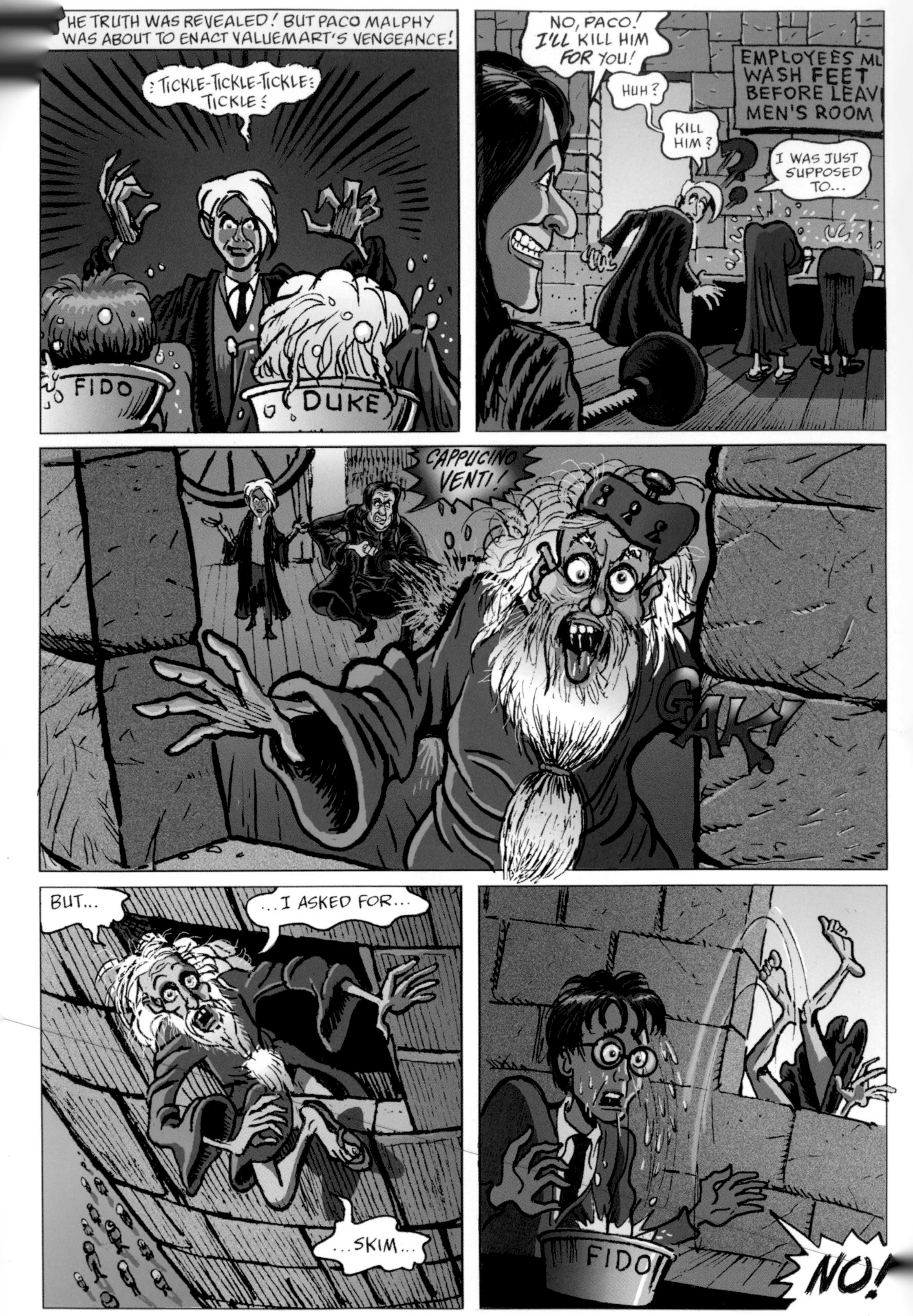
HE TRUTH WAS REVEALED! BUT PACO MALPHY WAS ABOUT TO ENACT VALUEMART'S VENGEANCE!
TICKLE-TICKLE-TICKLE TICKLE!
FIDO
DUKE
NO, PACO! I'LL KILL HIM FOR YOU!
EMPLOYEES M
WASH FEET
BEFORE LEAV
MEN'S ROOM
HUH?
KILL HIM?
I WAS JUST SUPPOSED TO...
CAPPUCINO VENTI!
GAK!
BUT...
...I ASKED FOR...
...SKIM...
FIDO
NO!

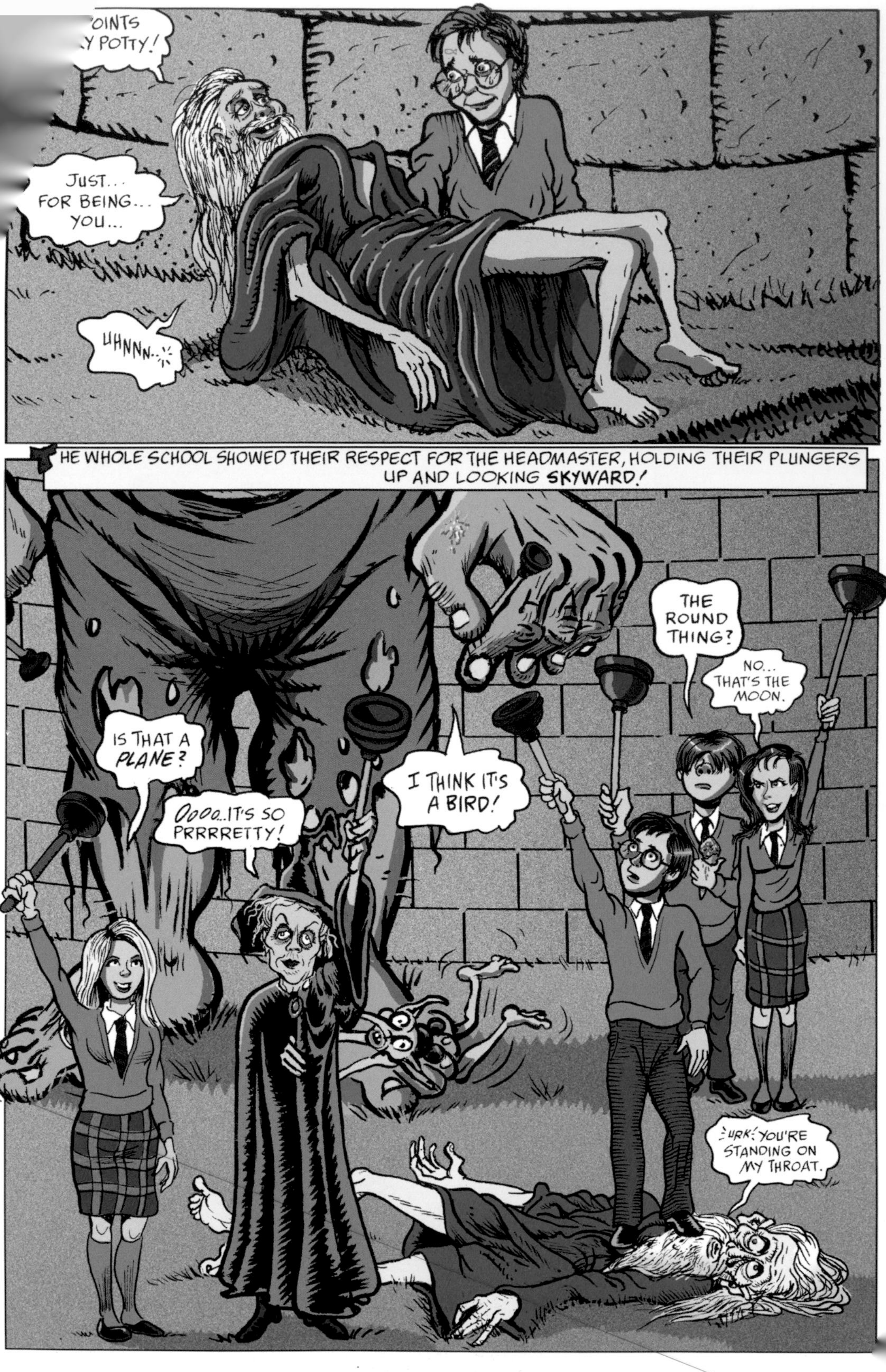
JUST... FOR BEING... YOU...
UHNNN...
HE WHOLE SCHOOL SHOWED THEIR RESPECT FOR THE HEADMASTER, HOLDING THEIR PLUNGERS UP AND LOOKING SKYWARD!
IS THAT A PLANE?
Oooo..IT'S SO PRRRRETTY!
I THINK IT'S A BIRD!
THE ROUND THING?
NO... THAT'S THE MOON.
URK! YOU'RE STANDING ON MY THROAT.

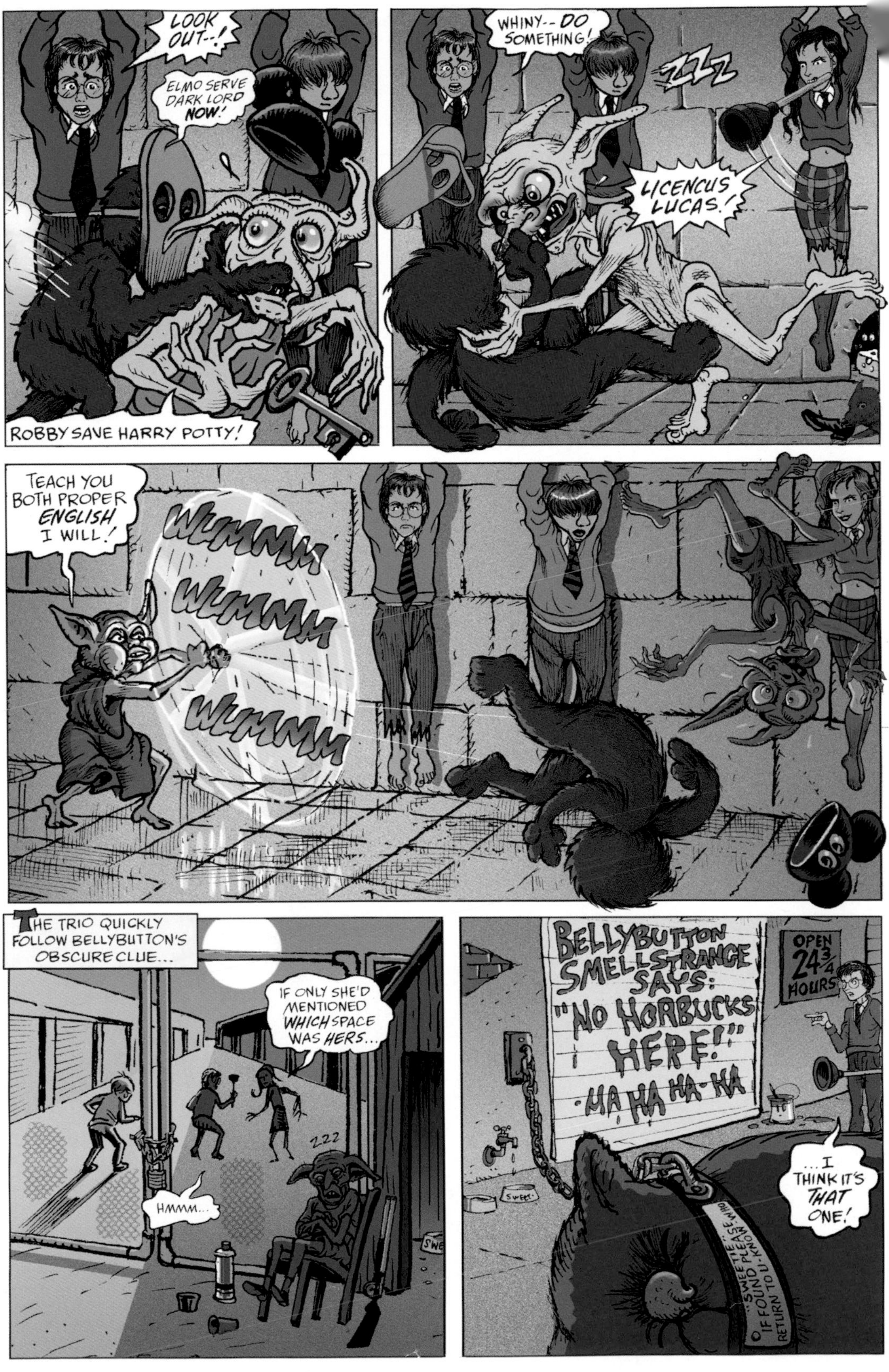

LOOK OUT--!
ELMO SERVE DARK LORD NOW!
ROBBY SAVE HARRY POTTY!
WHINY-- DO SOMETHING!
ZZZ
LICENCUS LUCAS!
TEACH YOU BOTH PROPER ENGLISH I WILL!
WUMMM
WUMMM
WUMMM
THE TRIO QUICKLY FOLLOW BELLYBUTTON'S OBSCURE CLUE...
IF ONLY SHE'D MENTIONED WHICH SPACE WAS HERS...
ZZZ
HMMM...
BELLYBUTTON SMELLSTRANGE SAYS: "NO HORBUCKS HERE!" HA HA HA-HA
OPEN 24 3/4 HOURS
SWEETIE
...I THINK IT'S THAT ONE!
"SWEETIE"
IF FOUND PLEASE
RETURN TO U-KNOW-WHO

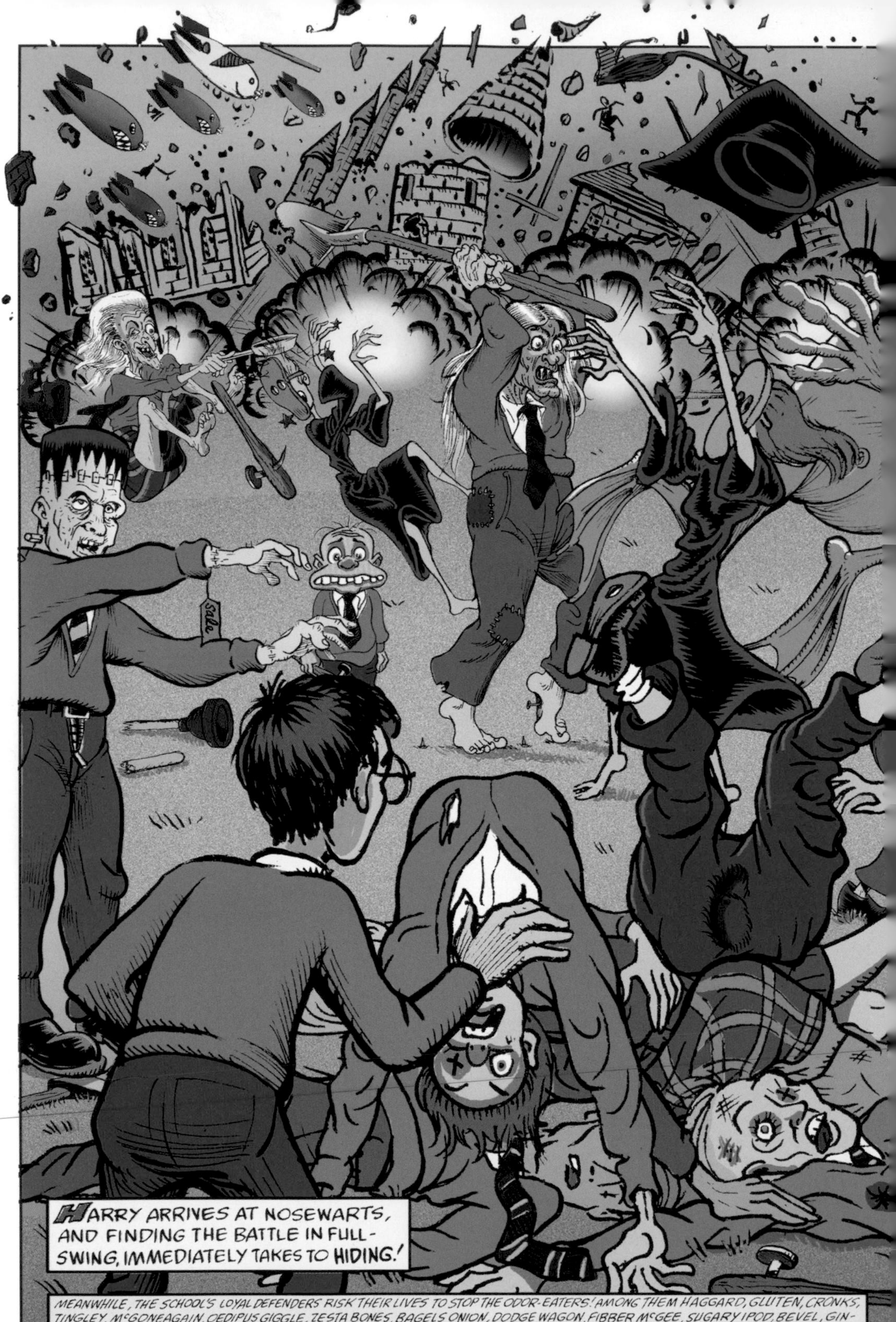
Sale
HARRY ARRIVES AT NOSEWARTS, AND FINDING THE BATTLE IN FULL-SWING, IMMEDIATELY TAKES TO HIDING!
MEANWHILE, THE SCHOOL'S LOYAL DEFENDERS RISK THEIR LIVES TO STOP THE ODOR-EATERS! AMONG THEM HAGGARD, GLUTEN, CRONKS, TINGLEY, McGONEAGAIN, OEDIPUS GIGGLE, ZESTA BONES, BAGELS ONION, DODGE WAGON, FIBBER McGEE, SUGARY IPOD, BEVEL, GIN-FIZZ, GED AND FORGE, HAVARTI, MUENSTER, iCARLY, THOMAS McMUFFIN, ANGELICA JOLIE, JUSTIN BIEBER, JAMES KIRK, LORNA DUNNE, CHOO-CHOO CHING, PADMY PILL, BARNABUS COLLINS, FLIPTICK, GROUT, BIG YAWNY, BUBBLY PLINK, MS. POMI, IRMA LaDUCE, MADAM HOOCHY-COOCHY, THE SNEECHES AND GLADYS KNIGHT AND THE PIPS!

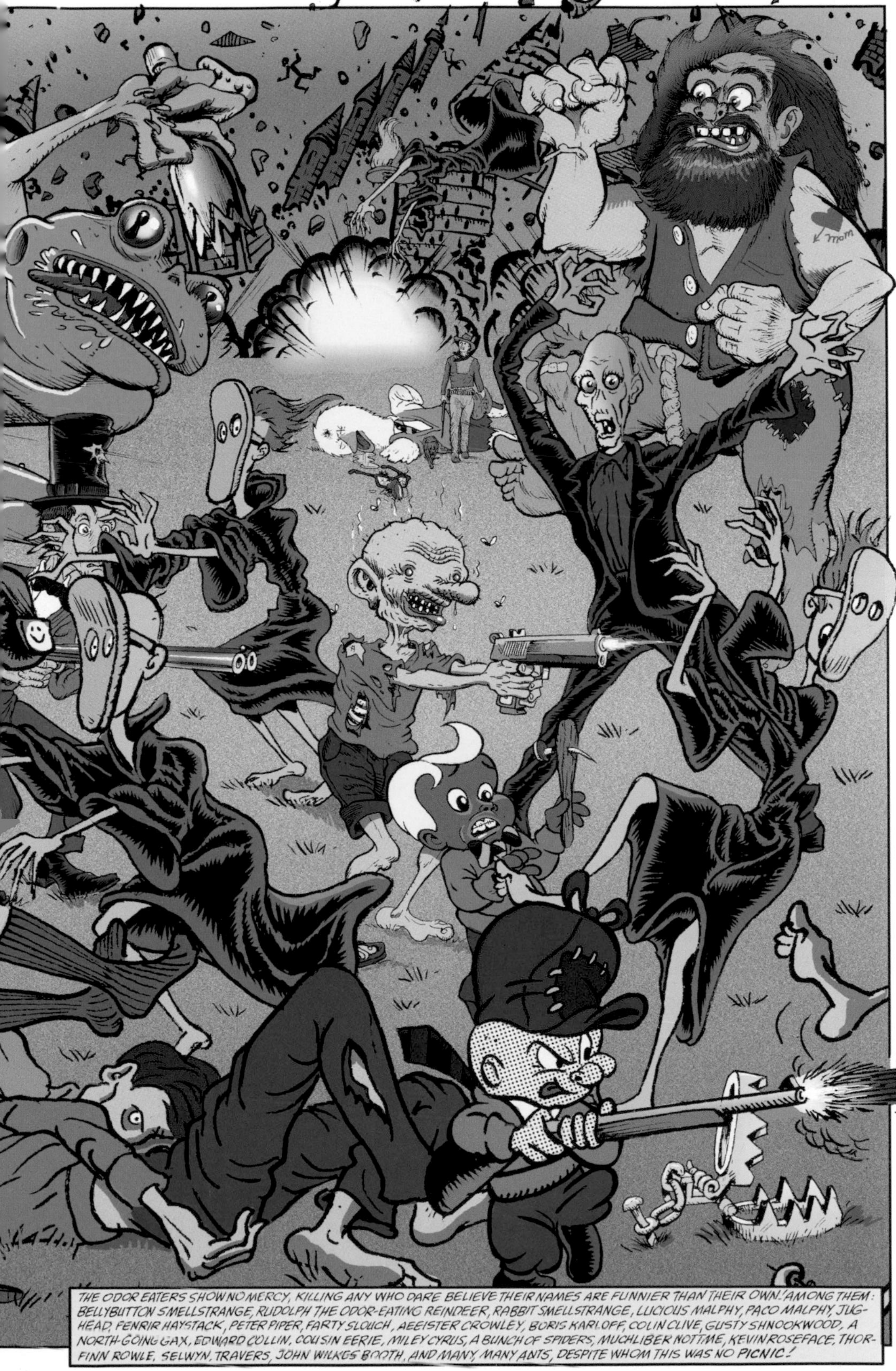
THE ODOR EATERS SHOW NO MERCY, KILLING ANY WHO DARE BELIEVE THEIR NAMES ARE FUNNIER THAN THEIR OWN! AMONG THEM: BELLYBUTTON SMELLSTRANGE, RUDOLPH THE ODOR-EATING REINDEER, RABBIT SMELLSTRANGE, LUCIOUS MALPHY, PACO MALPHY, JUG-HEAD, FENRIR HAYSTACK, PETER PIPER, FARTY SLOUCH, AEEISTER CROWLEY, BORIS KARLOFF, COLIN CLIVE, GUSTY SHNOOKWOOD, A NORTH-GOING GAX, EDWARD COLLIN, COUSIN EERIE, MILEY CYRUS, A BUNCH OF SPIDERS, MUCHLIBER NOTTME, KEVIN ROSEFACE, THOR-FINN ROWLE, SELWYN, TRAVERS, JOHN WILKES BOOTH, AND MANY, MANY ANTS, DESPITE WHOM THIS WAS NO PICNIC!

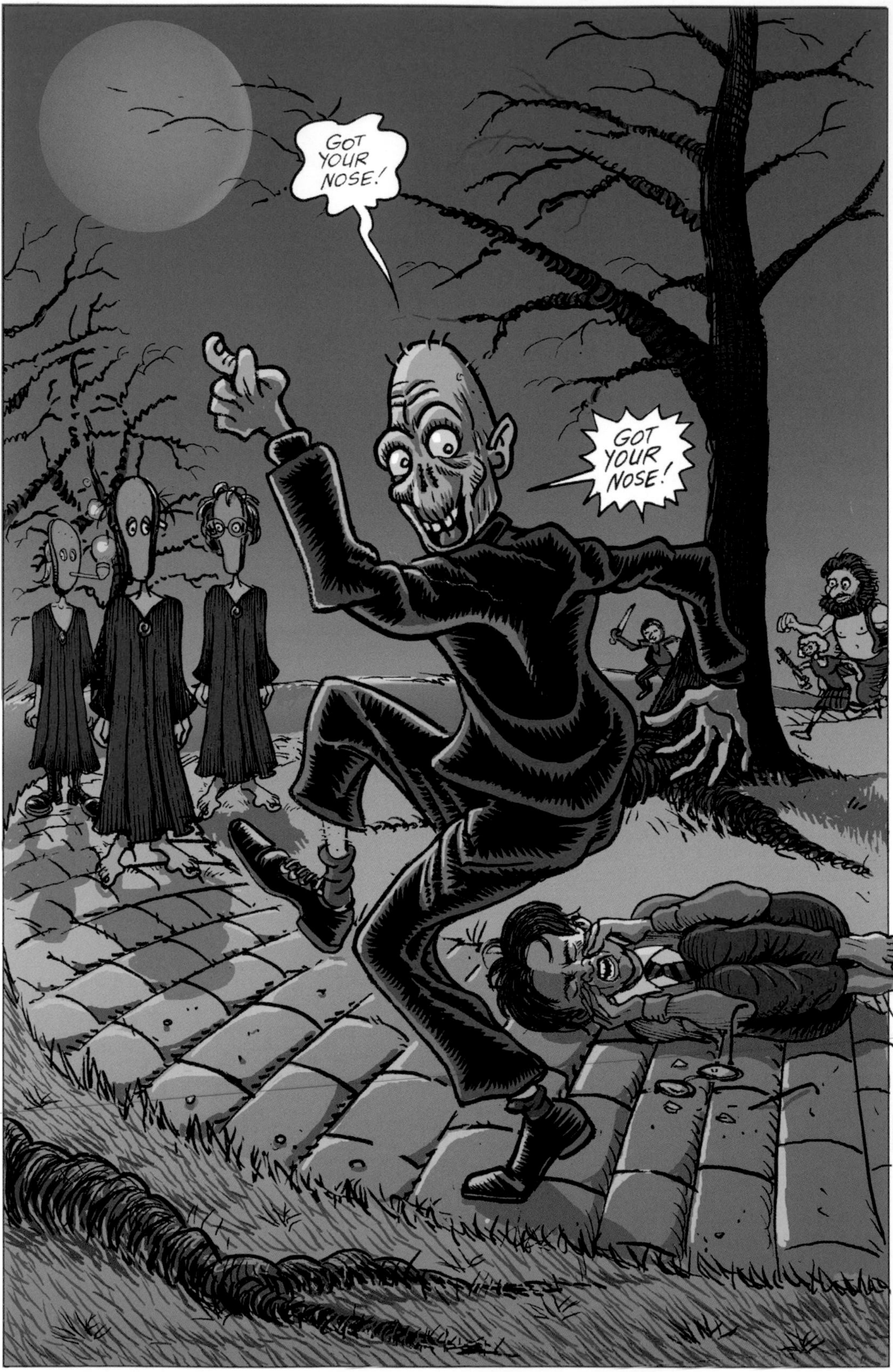
GOT YOUR NOSE!
GOT YOUR NOSE!

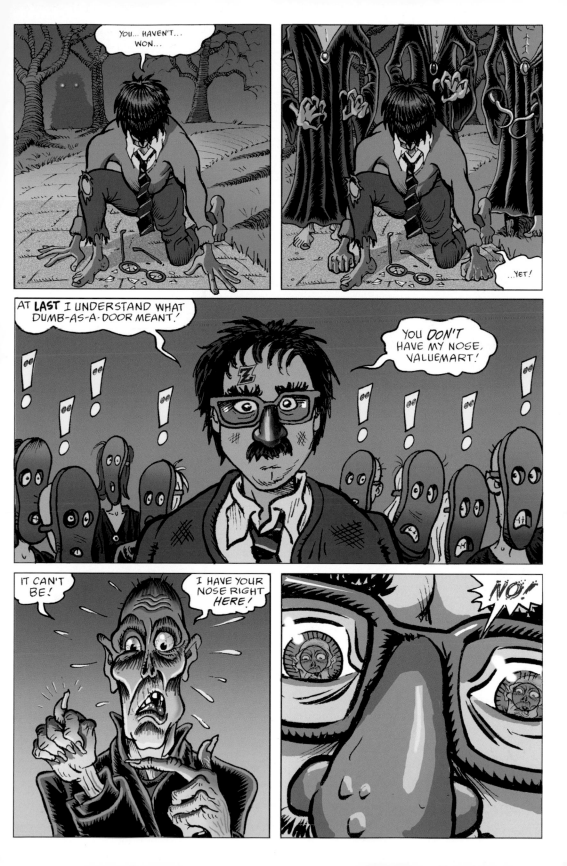

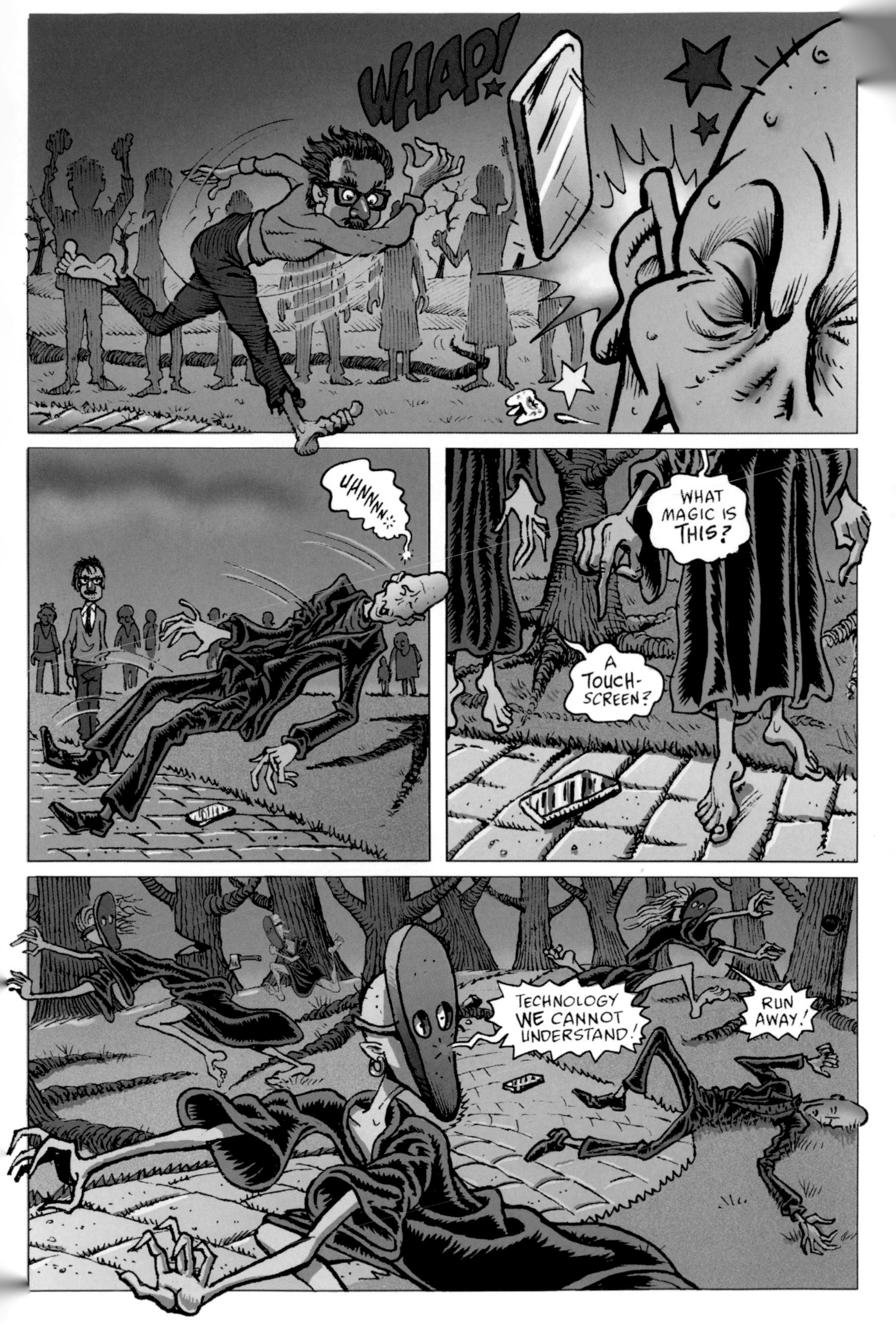
WHAP!
UHNNNN...!
WHAT MAGIC IS THIS?
A TOUCH-SCREEN?
TECHNOLOGY WE CANNOT UNDERSTAND!
RUN AWAY!

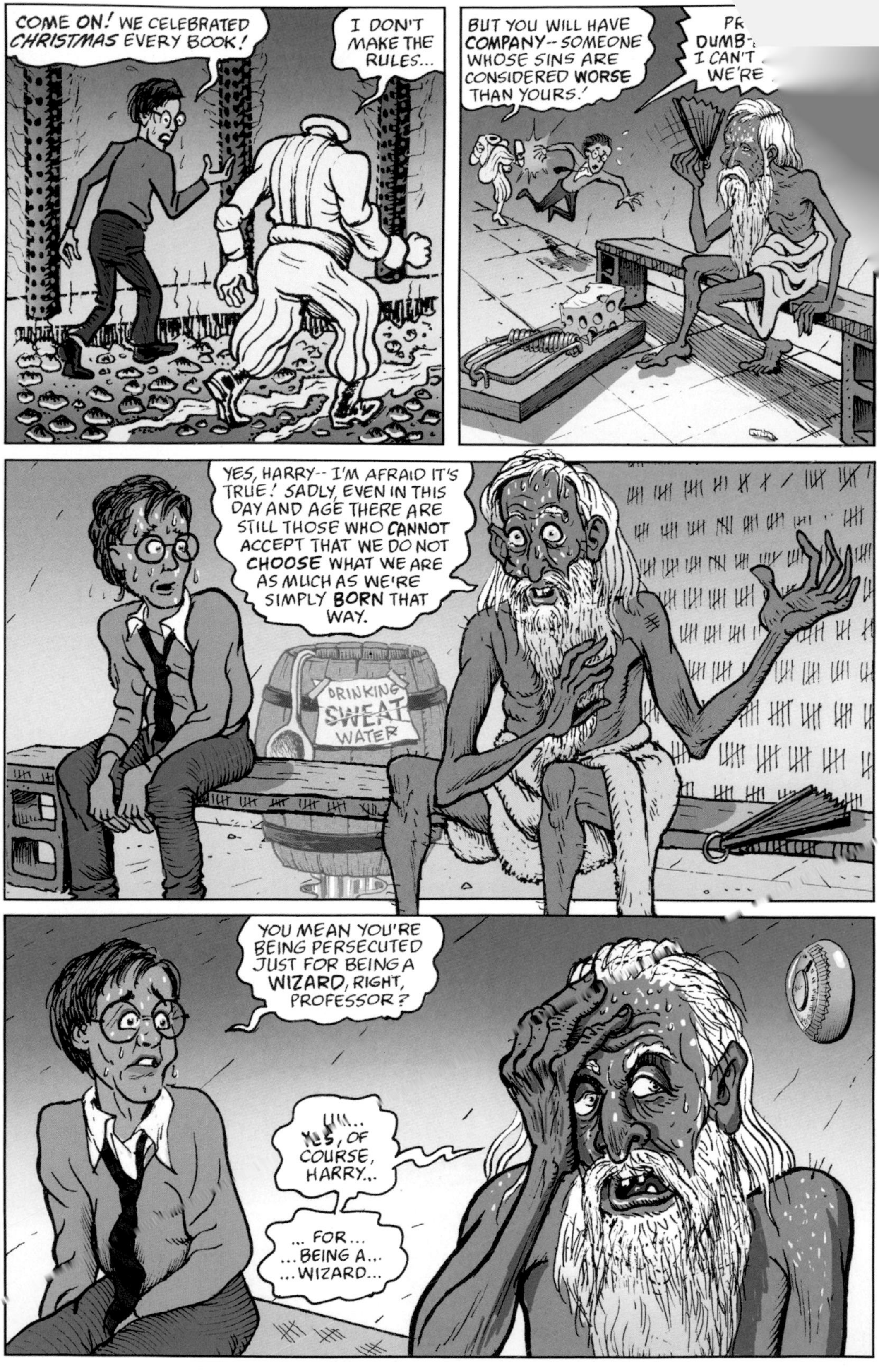
COME ON! WE CELEBRATED CHRISTMAS EVERY BOOK!
I DON'T MAKE THE RULES...
BUT YOU WILL HAVE COMPANY-- SOMEONE WHOSE SINS ARE CONSIDERED WORSE THAN YOURS!
PR
DUMB-
I CAN'T
WE'RE
YES, HARRY-- I'M AFRAID IT'S TRUE! SADLY, EVEN IN THIS DAY AND AGE THERE ARE STILL THOSE WHO CANNOT ACCEPT THAT WE DO NOT CHOOSE WHAT WE ARE AS MUCH AS WE'RE SIMPLY BORN THAT WAY.
DRINKING SWEAT WATER
YOU MEAN YOU'RE BEING PERSECUTED JUST FOR BEING A WIZARD, RIGHT, PROFESSOR?
UM.. YES, OF COURSE, HARRY..
... FOR... ...BEING A... ...WIZARD...

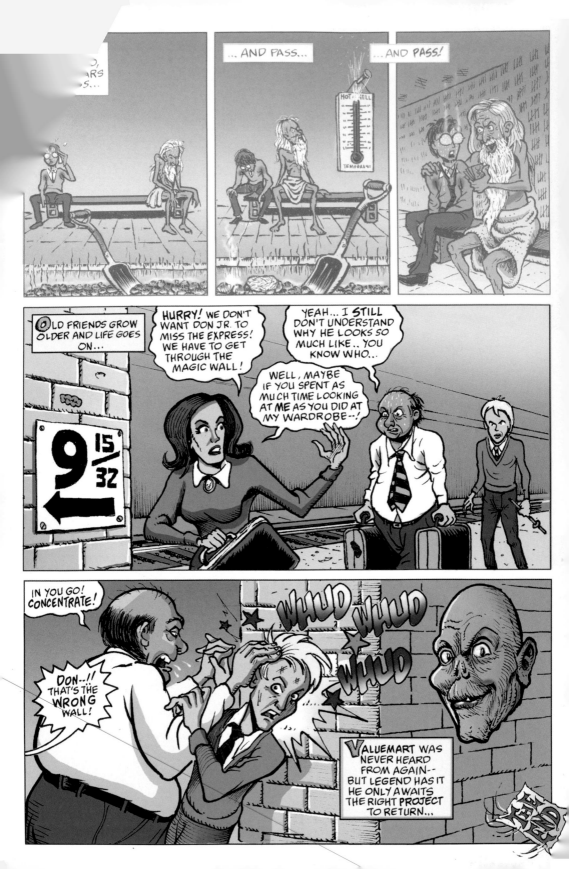

WATCH OUT FOR PAPERCUTZ ™

Welcome to the pun-filled premiere of PAPERCUTZ SLICES, the new graphic novel series dedicated to cutting up your favorite pop culture icons! I'm Jim Salicrup, your potty-trained Editor-in-Chief, here to provide a little behind-the scenes info on both Papercutz and PAPERCUTZ SLICES.

Papercutz, is the feisty, upstart graphic novel publisher which proudly brings you such incredible graphics novels such as BIONICLE, featuring all sorts of living robots with all sorts of funny names; CLASSICS ILLUSTRATED, the graphic novel series that takes great big novels and turns them into fast-paced comics (kinda like what's going on here in PAPERCUTZ SLICES, but not as funny); NANCY DREW, the sophisticated graphic novel series featuring America's favorite Girl Detective (and co-written by PAPERCUTZ SLICES's Stefan Petrucha), and TALES FROM THE CRYPT, the all-new graphic novel incarnation of the classic horror comic (with lots of contributions from Stefan as well as Rick Parker!). In other words, Papercutz is perhaps the most exciting, most-fun graphic novel publisher of all time, featuring comics by many of the greatest comics writers and artists ever. If you love comics, then you love Papercutz!

As for PAPERCUTZ SLICES, it's an all-new graphic novel series brought to you by writer Stefan Petrucha and artist Rick Parker. Stefan has been writing brilliant comics for years, featuring characters as diverse as Mickey Mouse, Spider-Man, Fox Mulder and Dana Skully, the Dana Girls (no relation), Duckman, Miracleman, and Lance Barnes, Post-Nuke Dick. He's also written equally brilliant novels such as *Making God*, *Teen Inc.*, *The Shadow of Frankenstein*, *The Rule of Won*, four volumes in the *Time Tripper* series, and more. Rick Parker has been drawing funny pictures since he was a little boy, and has drawn such insane comics as BEAVIS AND BUTT-HEAD and "Diary of a Stinky Dead Kid." In fact, it was on "Diary of a Stinky Dead Kid" that Stefan and Rick first worked together. Not only did that unauthorized parody in TALES FROM THE CRYPT #8 meet with critical acclaim, but it also became one of the biggest selling graphic novels from Papercutz.

It didn't take long before Stefan was suggesting that Papercutz should consider an ongoing graphic novel filled with same kind of pop culture parodies, and just like that PAPERCUTZ SLICES was born (Hey! We're no dummies!) Stefan also insisted on starting off with "Harry Potty and the Deathly Boring," and again we think he was 100% correct! Let us know what you think—email me at salicrup@papercutz or send your snailmail to PAPERCUTZ SLICES, 40 Exchange Place, Suite 1308, New York, NY 10005. We may run the most interesting (or dumbest) comments in PAPERCUTZ SLICES #2.

In the meantime, check out the all-new follow-up to "Diary of a Stinky Dead Kid" in TALES FROM THE CRYPT #9 "Wickeder," on sale now. It's written by Stefan Petrucha (and daughter Margo Kinney-Petrucha) and drawn by Diego Jourdan, who drew the very first picture of Glugg, the Stinky Dead Kid for the cover of TALES FROM THE CRYPT #8. For a special sneak preview—just keep turning the pages, you'll find it soon enough!

So that's it for now. Be sure to come back for PAPERCUTZ SLICES #2 "Breaking Down"! If you can't figure out what we'll be spoofing based on the title, here's a big clue-- an actual quote from author Stephenie Meyer: "I'm burned out on vampires right now." So are we, but that just makes lampooning shiny vampires that much more fun!

Thanks,

Jim

PRESENTING AN ALL-NEW SERIES FROM PAPERCUTZ...

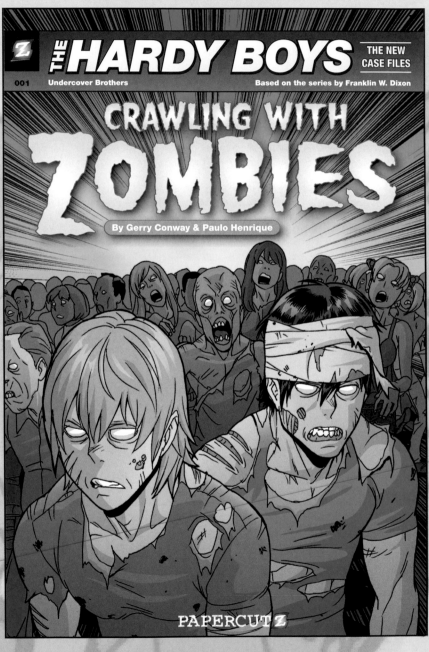

COMING FALL 2010!

DON'T MISS TALES FROM THE CRYPT #9 "WICKEDER"
ON SALE EVERYWHERE!

The Stinky Dead Kid Returns In...

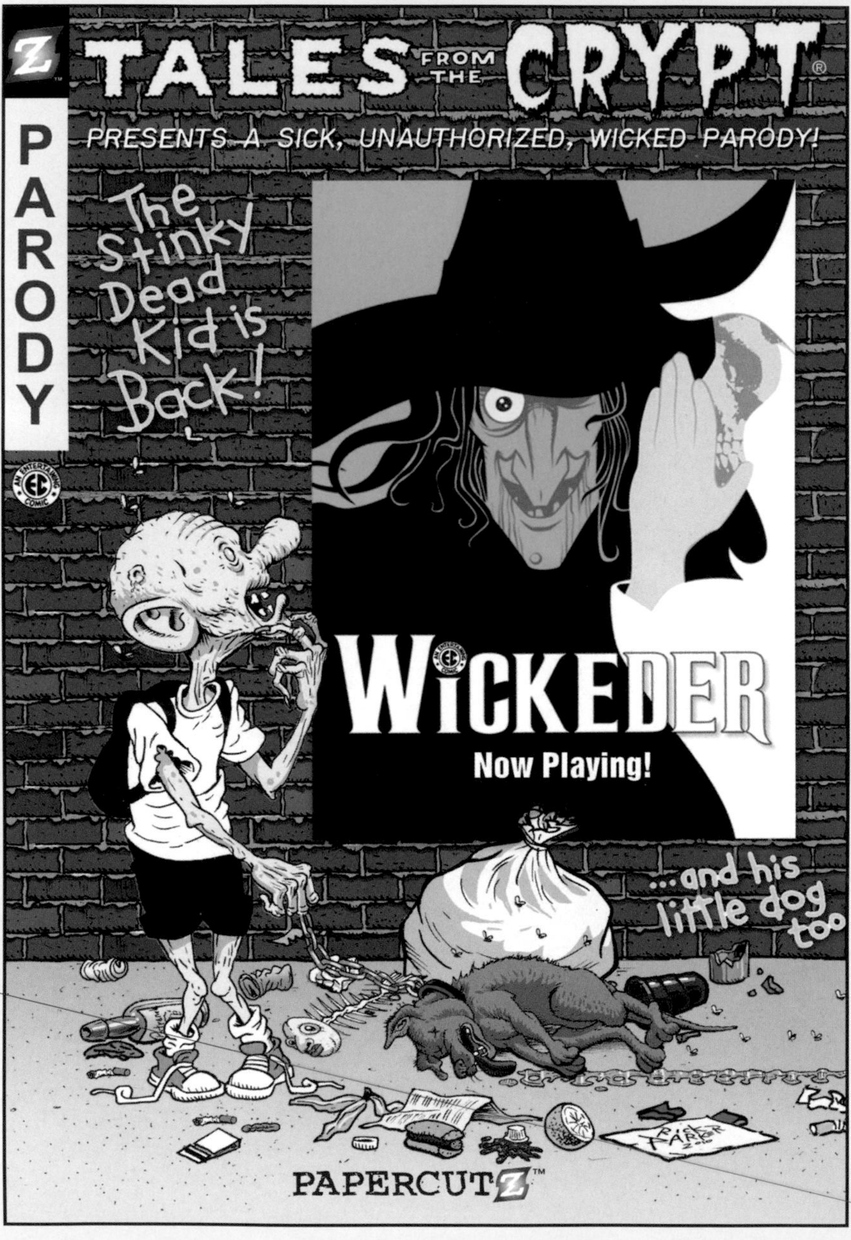
TALES FROM THE CRYPT®
PRESENTS A SICK, UNAUTHORIZED, WICKED PARODY!
PARODY
The Stinky Dead Kid is Back!
WICKEDER
Now Playing!
...and his little dog too
PAPERCUTZ™

Coming Fall 2010!